Praise for N... The Fo...

A Junior Library Guild selection

An International Thriller Writers Thriller Award Nominee for Best YA Novel

"[*The Forgetting*] will leave you wanting more from Maggi!"

—Gretchen McNeil, author of *Ten* and the Don't Get Mad series

"From the tender moments to the thrilling climax, this one will keep your heart racing."

—Natalie D. Richards, author of *Six Months Later* and *We All Fall Down*

"A powerful call to action."

—*Kirkus Reviews*

"Sheds light on an important social justice issue not often addressed in YA fiction."

—*School Library Journal*

Also by Nicole Maggi

The Forgetting

WHAT THEY *don't* KNOW

NICOLE MAGGI

Cover design by Whitney Manger
Cover images © Karina Vegas/Arcangel; Ajintai/Shutterstock; r.kathesi/Shutterstock
Internal design by Travis Hasenour/Sourcebooks, Inc.
Internal images © Stephen Rees/Thinkstock; everythingpossible/Thinkstock; DavidMSchrader/Thinkstock

Published by Sourcebooks Fire, an imprint of Sourcebooks, Inc.
P.O. Box 4410, Naperville, Illinois 60567-4410
(630) 961-3900
Fax: (630) 961-2168
sourcebooks.com

Library of Congress Cataloging-in-Publication Data

Names: Maggi, Nicole, author.
Title: What they don't know / Nicole Maggi.
Other titles: What they do not know
Description: Naperville, Illinois : Sourcebooks Fire, [2018] | Summary: Alternating journal entries chronicle the powerful fight for Mellie's right to choose after she becomes pregnant by rape.
Identifiers: LCCN 2018010647 | (pbk. : alk. paper)
Subjects: | CYAC: Pregnancy--Fiction. | Abortion--Fiction. | Family life--Fiction. | Rape--Fiction. | Christian life--Fiction. | Diaries--Fiction.
Classification: LCC PZ7.1.M33 Wh 2018 | DDC [Fic]--dc23 LC record available at https://lccn.loc.gov/2018010647

Printed and bound in Canada.
MBP 10 9 8 7 6 5 4 3 2 1

In memory of my mother

and for all the women who came before

to pave the way

February 13

Dear Ms. Tilson,

You probably think you know who I am, but I'm here to tell you that you don't. I used to be a bright star of a girl, but that girl burned out of existence, like a fire swept through my life and left nothing but ash and smoke. That smoke is the memory of what I had, so thick I can smell it and feel it in my eyes and ears and nose. But I can't touch it. Smoke, like memories, will slip through your fingers and disappear as if it never existed at all.

I keep thinking that if I could write down how my life used to be, maybe I could capture that smoke, keep it from drifting away. That's what made me finally crack open this journal you gave us at the beginning of the semester. Could these pages be some magical vessel to contain that gone-girl? All those bright memories preserved in this one place?

I would write about how on Sundays, after the long hours spent at church, we'd pile into the truck, exhausted, and my mom would say, "I'm too tired to cook," which is the greatest sin for a woman on a Sunday in our church, but my dad would smile indulgently and order a pizza. "God rested on Sunday; why shouldn't you?" he'd joke. Then they would kiss, and I'd be reminded that I'm one of six kids, so they must've had sex at some point. Which is gross to think about but also comforting because it means there's some order to the world.

I'd write about how when my youngest sister, Joanie, was a baby and would wake up crying in the middle of the night, I was usually the one who got there first with a bottle of warmed-up breast milk from the freezer. Some nights I'd rock her for hours even after she'd fallen asleep, watching her tiny eyelids flutter as she dreamed. *What is she dreaming about?* I'd wonder. Sometimes I'd place her gently in her crib and get my sketchbook, draw her in soft, black pencil. Those nights were magical. They seemed to exist in their own dimension, the spell broken only by the rising sun.

I'd write about the day after my older sister, Hannah, got her license. She picked me up from school, and instead of going straight home, we drove and drove and drove. We rode over the mountain passes, twisting along back roads until we came to this hole-in-the-wall dive in the middle of nowhere called the Wooden Nickel. Hannah had read about it in *Sunset Magazine*, how it supposedly had the best bison burgers in America. We ate them with their secret special sauce dripping down our chins, washed them down with small-batch root beer, and got home hours after dark. Mom and Dad yelled their heads off, and Hannah lost her license for a week, but after they sent us to bed, Hannah turned to me and said, "Worth it."

I'd write about how I had everything I wanted and didn't know it. I had a family who surrounded me with love and acceptance. I had a father and mother who stood on such high pedestals that the sun blinded me when I looked up at them. They loved me unconditionally, or so I thought. I never imagined there could be conditions under which they would not love me.

Every night I thanked God for my parents' love and for my family's abundance, and yet every day I took each of those things for granted. Now I'm left with the memory of what I once had.

No. These pages can't contain that smoke, those memories. They're gone now, destroyed in one irreversible moment.

Maybe I should stop here. Let you go on believing everything you think you know about me. That would definitely be easiest. I could record what I ate for breakfast, what time I went to bed, which TV shows I like to watch. All those myths you have about me can stay intact. You can go on thinking I'm the perfect daughter of Mayor Rivers, the shining example of the family values he talks about in speech after speech after speech. Believe that I never cause any trouble and I'm always a good girl. I'll probably get a C, but you'll never know my innermost thoughts. I'll stay safe.

Except I can't stay safe anymore.

As of December 21, nowhere is safe.

I would give anything to redo that day.

But I can't.

And the only place I can talk about it is in these pages.

So let's start with a pop quiz. TRUE or FALSE: Mellie Rivers is a virgin.

False. As of December 21, at 3:30 in the afternoon, on the floor in the basement of my house, I am not a virgin.

TRUE or FALSE: Mellie Rivers would never have sex before marriage.

True. I made a promise to God and my family, and I wear the ring on my left hand, where, presumably, one day, my husband will place a different, more permanent ring. I would have kept that promise. But the choice was taken from me.

TRUE or FALSE: Mellie Rivers would never, *ever* get pregnant out of wedlock.

False.

Signed,

Mellie Rivers

February 13

Dear Ms. Tilson—

Mom always tells me that I can do anything I put my mind to, but sometimes I think she's lying.

Okay, maybe not *lying*, because I don't think my mom ever intentionally lies to me, but maybe she's being overly optimistic. She's not accounting for the fact that sometimes the universe doesn't want you to do everything you put your mind to. Sometimes, in fact, the world pits itself against you so that no matter how hard you try, you're gonna fail.

Today the world—okay, the school board, but it feels like the world—pitted itself against me and I failed. And it feels like crap. Which is why I'm writing this from under a fluffy blanket on the couch with *Parks and Recreation* on in the background because Leslie Knope always cheers me up.

They suck. The school board, I mean. It didn't matter that I had a petition with 250 signatures, the backing of both guidance counselors, and a bunch of the teachers (including you, thank you for that) supporting a gender-neutral dress code. They just went on and on about MORALS and VALUES and DECENCY. The not-so-subtle subtext was that girls are sexual temptresses and boys must be protected from them.

Because if you read the stupid dress code that's been in place since, like, the late 1700s, it doesn't say anything about what boys can and can't wear. It doesn't prohibit shorts for boys. Just for girls. It doesn't prohibit tank tops for boys. Just for girls.

The dress code doesn't give hemline or neckline or strap-width restrictions for whatever boys want to wear to prom. No, only girls are subject to that. Those red T-shirts that Principal Conway keeps in her office for when someone violates the dress code only come in girls' sizes. We're the ones who are forced to wear those shirts—like we're straight out of freaking Gilead—when we have the gall to show a bra strap. Because, OH MY GOD, how dare we remind anyone that girls have breasts and wear bras?

Superintendent Fugelson (I really want to write a mean perversion of his name, but I will restrain myself) actually had the nerve to say that the dress code was for "our own good." Because, you know, a boy could get the wrong idea if a girl wears a spaghetti strap that's narrower than half an inch. A boy might lose control if the neckline of a girl's shirt is too low. And that, of course, would be the girl's fault for wearing said shirt in the first place.

I wish I could say that I'm shocked, but I'm not. I didn't really expect the school board to lose its misogynistic worldview overnight. But I had this seed of hope inside me that I let take root. I thought that maybe, just maybe, if I was passionate enough, if I gave a really well-reasoned argument, and had the support of the students and staff, the board would see that I was right. That this wasn't the whim of some silly girl, but a serious cause from a serious thinker.

Instead, the school board made me feel like the Whore of Babylon for wanting to wear a dress that hit above my knee and sent me home with my tail between my legs.

And you know what the worst part is? I felt ashamed. Ashamed for asking for something so small. Ashamed for wanting to be valued the same as the boys in my school. Ashamed for speaking up for myself. Like I was naughty for raising my voice in a room where I'm meant to be silent.

On the way out of the meeting, I could feel the tears welling up inside me. I had to run into the bathroom before they fell. I hunched over the sink and cried until my eyes were red and swollen, and then I had to put on a ton of powder to look even halfway normal. That's how low they made me feel. I hate that I let them make me feel that way.

You know what? NO. I'm not going to give them that power. I'm going to keep using my voice. I'll raise it, and I'll keep raising it until I get so loud they can't ignore me.

—Lise

February 14
Afternoon
Dear Ms. Tilson,

I'm sitting in study hall, surrounded by roses. The Valentine's Day roses the student government sells as a fund-raiser are everywhere. Everyone sends flowers to each other, not just boyfriends and girlfriends, but friends too. If you send a rose to one friend and not another, you're saying something about that friendship, so if you're a decent person, you send them to everyone in your circle.

That's what I did, anyway. White for all my friends (except Delia, who got pink because she's my best friend, so she deserves a special rose). Of course, I got roses in return, mostly white, but a couple of pink ones too, and a deep red rose from Delia with a little note attached.

I love you so much, Mellie! I can't wait to be sisters-in-law!

I can't stop staring at her note.

It's like trying to catch that smoke in my hands again.

I wanted to write something sweet and cheery to Delia too. I wanted to write about the night Hannah got engaged. It was at the church BBQ last summer. The fireflies were twinkling all around us, and the first people Delia and I hugged after we heard the news weren't my sister or her brother, but each other, because we'd achieved what all best friends want. We were becoming actual sisters.

I wanted to write about how we jumped up and down, screaming so loud that Delia's dad finally yelled at us to stop, and Hannah stomped her foot and said, "Aren't you going to congratulate *me*?" I could have written a three-page letter about everything Delia and I have done together, about how we know each other so well that we're already like sisters, how we don't need a marriage certificate to make it legal. I wanted to write about all the secrets we've shared, like how she puts on makeup when she gets to school and then washes it off before she goes home, or how she knows I read all the Harry Potter books behind my parents' backs even though my dad disapproves of them. It means so much to me that she can trust me with her secrets, and I can trust her with mine.

Oh, I wanted to tell her all that so bad.

But I couldn't.

Because now I have a secret that I can't tell her.

I want to trust her.

But I can't risk it. Delia likes to see herself above everyone else. We've always been equals, but I think if I tell her this, she'll look down on me, like she does the rest of our friends. I'll no longer be on her level.

I couldn't stand that.

I've lost so much already. I don't want to lose her respect too.

So I wrote: *Happy Valentine's Day to my bestie!*

And the rose was pink. Not red.

I wonder what roses I'll get next year.

When everyone finds out what happened, who will still love me?

Signed,
Mellie Rivers

February 14
Dear Ms. Tilson,

I threw away the roses when I got home. I put them in the green bin outside so no one would ask why I was getting rid of perfectly good flowers.

Delia's was on top. The red petals fell off, splayed against the white.

I slammed the lid to hide them. The red petals looked like blood.

There was blood on my thighs after it happened.

And now there's no blood, which is even worse.

You're probably wondering if I reported what happened. I did not. Now you're asking yourself why, right? Maybe I imagined it. Maybe I didn't say no loud enough. Maybe it was my fault.

That's why I didn't report it.

I didn't want everyone questioning me. Doubting me. And mostly, I wanted to forget that it happened. I stopped going down into the basement. If my mother asked me to deal with the laundry or get an extra jar of tomato sauce, I got one of my sisters to do it. If I didn't go down there, then it was easier to pretend it didn't happen.

I've been so wrapped up in this cocoon of *It didn't happen* that I didn't notice time passing. Days blurred together. Saturday was indistinguishable from Tuesday, and a math test that I think happened on a Thursday could very well have been a Monday.

So it wasn't until a couple of days ago, when I stared at February stretched out below DaVinci's *Virgin of the Rocks* in our Women of the Bible calendar that I noticed.

Eight weeks.

Eight weeks since it happened.

But actually…ten weeks.

Ten weeks since my last period.

My mother has spent a lot of my life either pregnant or trying to get pregnant. Since Joanie was born six years ago, she's been trying to get pregnant one last time, hoping for that elusive second boy. Instead, she's had two miscarriages.

Because of this, I know she has pregnancy tests in her bathroom. After dinner, I made sure everyone was occupied with dishes or homework or basketball on the television, and I snuck upstairs into my parents' bedroom, to their private bathroom. I searched through a couple of drawers before I found two boxes of pregnancy tests. One was open and the other was still sealed.

The opened box had one test left in it. My hand hovered over the drawer. If I took the last one, would she notice it was missing? How long ago had she taken the other test? And then there was the question of what to do with the empty box. I couldn't throw it away at home, but I also couldn't risk hiding it in my bag, where one of my sisters might see it.

I swallowed hard. Precious time was slipping away. I couldn't get caught in my parents' bathroom. I am not supposed to go into their private space. So I snatched the test and pushed the empty box to the back of the drawer, hoping that if my mother saw it, she would think she'd forgotten to throw out the box. Sliding the test into the waistband of my skirt, I dashed out of the bathroom, past their big king bed, and down the hall to the bathroom I share with my sisters.

"What were you doing in Mom and Dad's room?"

I whirled around. Hannah stood at the top of the stairs, her gaze shifting between me and the door to my parents' room. I couldn't look her in the eye. "I…I needed a tissue, and we're out in our bathroom. In fact," I said, raising my voice, "can you run down to the basement and grab a box?"

"Sure." Hannah gave me another narrow-eyed look, then turned back down the stairs.

Without breathing, I made it to my bathroom and locked myself inside. Thankfully, we actually were out of tissues, but I only had a few minutes until Hannah would come knocking on the door. I ripped off the wrapping, hitched up my skirt, pulled down my underwear, and crouched over the toilet to pee on the stick.

Two minutes.

I had to wait two minutes.

The last eight weeks passed in a blurry haze, but those two minutes felt like the longest of my life.

Two minutes in which all I could think about was what if… What if I hadn't gone down into the basement that day? What if I'd locked the door behind me, or brought a knife down there with me?

Two minutes and a lifetime later, a bright fuchsia plus sign appeared. It only took two minutes for everything I've ever known, everything I've ever believed, to be destroyed.

I hope you never have two minutes like that in your life.

Signed,
Mellie Rivers

February 14
Late (midnight, maybe?)
Dear Ms. Tilson,

I'm lying in bed, and I see my life spill out before me like a knocked-over glass of grape juice that I'm desperately trying to sop up before it reaches the white carpet. It's slipping away from me, and my fingers aren't fast enough to stop it before it makes a mess.

I see my stomach growing, past the point where I can hide it. I see myself walking through the halls of school, students clearing out of my way. Don't get too close to the pregnant girl. It's contagious.

I hear myself saying those words to Mom and Dad: "I'm pregnant." The whole conversation unfolds in my head. I know exactly how it will go. Mom will cry. Dad will grow tight-faced, his lips white, anger like a tidal wave until it gives way to disappointment and then acceptance. "Well, we'll just have to deal with it, won't we?"

They will ask who the father is. And I will lie. Because even if I told the truth—even if they *believed* the truth—it would still somehow be my fault. So I'll wear this pregnancy like a badge of dishonor and become a living, breathing cautionary tale. This is what happens to you if you're not careful.

And then I'll have the baby.

The juice reaches the carpet and stains it purple.

I imagine the nurse putting a baby in my arms, screaming, red-faced, every cry a reminder of what happened in that basement.

And Baby will grow up, and one day he'll ask, "What was my daddy like?"

How many lies will I have to tell for the rest of my life?

He will have won. He will have seeped his way into every fiber of my life, staining everything that was once clean.

I can feel myself sinking and I haven't even lived this life yet. But this is it. It's already been decided, right? I don't have a choice.

Do I?

Signed,

Mellie Rivers

February 14
Dear Ms. Tilson—

Sometimes the smallest things can break you. It can be completely innocuous, but the littlest detail can catch you, wreck your heart and your soul.

Something like that happens to me every time I volunteer at the clinic.

I'm only allowed to volunteer once a week, and since I started volunteering the day I turned sixteen, I've never missed a week. There weren't a lot of appointments—no one wants to go to the doctor's on Valentine's Day unless they absolutely have to—but there are always protesters outside, no matter what day it is. I guess they have nothing better to do than tell someone what she should and shouldn't do with her own body.

Maybe it's a bad idea to write about this. Maybe it's too controversial. But you said to share our innermost thoughts, and while there are some I have to keep safe from everyone, there are some that I can't keep in. There are some that fill me with so much rage I have to put it somewhere, so I'm trusting you to keep this safe. You said you were trustworthy when you handed out these journals. I hope that's true.

Most of the women I escorted in and out of the clinic today weren't there for abortions. I know this, because many of them told me on their way in. "I'm only here for a mammogram," they murmured as I held their arms and navigated briskly past the line of protesters.

I've come to know the protesters. Not by name, by their actions. There's the one I call Hail Mary, because she says the rosary over and over again, really loud, as she paces the line, her wooden rosary beads working their way through her fingers as she recites. There's Bible Thumper, who pounds on his Bible as he screams at the top of his lungs about the sanctity of life and how motherhood is the only true path for women. And there's the one I think of as You Could Die Tomorrow, because he goes on and on about how we could die tomorrow and we should atone for our sins before that happens so we don't rot in hell. He likes to get real close to me, as close as the law allows, and talk about how my soul will be damned for what I'm doing. It takes all my strength not to punch him in the face, so much so that my body shakes from the effort of not decking him.

"Don't engage," I tell the women I escort. It's a reflex. *Don't engage.* That was drilled into me during my escort training. It doesn't matter whether you're here for a mammogram or a Pap smear or to get a refill for your birth control or to terminate a pregnancy. These people don't care. All they see are women giving their business to a place they think is a baby-killing factory. I've seen Bible Thumper get into a screaming match with a bald woman who was clearly going through chemotherapy and not pregnant at all. They don't give a shit. They want to hear their own voices drown out everyone else's.

"They should be praying that I don't have cancer," one woman said to me when I got her inside the door. I forced a smile. The crowd was starting to get to me, and I still had an hour left of my shift. Jasmine, the security guard, could see it. She handed me a Snickers bar and squeezed my arm.

Jasmine is the only one of us who is allowed to engage, because it's her job to protect the clinic and its patients by any means necessary. It takes a special kind of person to be a security guard at an abortion clinic. I've seen her stand outside her guard post, outside of its bulletproof glass, her tiny, wiry body its own fierce wall, and recite that famous quote from the nun who called out the "pro-life" movement for its hypocrisy. You know the one, about how if you don't want your tax dollars going to health care or education for children, then you can't call yourself pro-life, you're only pro-birth. Jasmine spoke in such a calm, authoritative tone, like she was giving a speech on a podium, that she completely shut down those protesters. In fact, most of them packed up and left a little while later.

I wish I had that ability. I try so hard to stay calm but the anger just bubbles up inside me. These people are such hypocrites, squawking about how the government shouldn't intrude on people's lives one minute and then preaching the need for the most intrusive law—telling a woman what to do with her own body—the next. I am not like Jasmine. All my reasoned logic flies out of my brain, and I want to scream curses at them.

When I did my training, I told the counselor I was afraid I'd lose my shit on protesters while volunteering. She looked at me and said, "You can lose your shit. Just do it when you get home." I'm proud to say I've never lost my shit at the clinic. Instead, I absorb all the anger, and I carry it with me until I get home.

But by the time I get home, I'm not angry anymore. I'm sad, sad down to my bones. Sad that this is what women have to deal with, women who simply want to make sure they don't have breast cancer or who want to prevent pregnancy or get a checkup to make sure they're healthy. Yes, some want to terminate a pregnancy, which they have a legal right to do in a safe, clean place. The government can shut down every clinic in the world, but abortions are still going to happen. And then where does that leave us? In back alleyways with rusty coat hangers?

So I take all of this emotion home with me, and I break in

places I didn't know I had. I curl up on the couch or my bed and not even *Parks and Rec* can make me feel better, not even the episode where Leslie Knope teaches a bunch of senior citizens how to use condoms.

When Mom sees me like this, she tells me to stop. She tells me to quit volunteering at the clinic. "It's too much," she says. "I hate what it's doing to you."

But I can't stop. I won't stop.

Because even though it is hard, it's the only thing I do that means something. I know that school and all the other activities I'm involved in aren't meaningless, but all that pales in comparison to what I do at the clinic. It's the only thing that makes me feel like I'm doing something important.

Today, the one woman who was actually there to have an abortion collapsed crying in my arms when we reached the safety of the front door. That's how I knew why she was there. She didn't tell me; she didn't have to. It was written all over her face. This choice—it's so hard on women, and those despicable people make it a thousand times more terrible. They have NO IDEA what these women go through. But I do. I see it. I feel it in the way they clutch my hand as we walk past the posters with pictures of aborted fetuses.

That's why I'll never stop. Not until there are no protesters and women can walk into that clinic with their heads held high because they're supported every step of the way. I don't care if it weighs on me. Because if walking them into the clinic is hard for me, what is it like for the women I'm escorting in?

I wish I could take away some of their pain. If I had a superpower, I'd want to absorb all that pain and turn it into something bright and beautiful.

Something to change the world.

—Lise

February 15
Early morning
Dear Ms. Tilson,

Last night, when I finally fell asleep, I dreamed of Baby.

Baby crying all night long.

Baby biting me and laughing.

Baby being exactly like his father.

I woke up sweating, tears streaming down my cheeks.

This is not the life I chose. But how can I stop it?

I'll be stuck in this house forever, needing Mom's help long past when I should've moved out. I wonder what Baby will call her. Grammy? Or Mom Number Two?

I try to imagine when Baby will be three or six or eleven. Will I ever be able to look at him without seeing HIM? In my head, Baby is a him, like HIM. Will I be haunted by those terrible, awful minutes in the basement every time I look at his child?

My insides twist as I write that, white-hot rage and cold

dread tangled together. The pain is so intense that my heart hurts, like, physically aches. Can I do that? Live with that pain every single day? Relive the worst moment of my life whenever I look at that child?

They say that Hell looks different for everyone. That for some people it's burning in eternal fires and for others it's being trapped in a small room with no escape. I know what my Hell looks like.

It looks like being Baby's mother.

Living every day with the reminder of how he raped me.

I want to scream, throw a glass across the room and watch it shatter, slice my skin to let out the pain. Why? Why *me*? Why should I be the one to live that Hell? *He's* the one who did something wrong. Why do I have to be punished for it?

I can't do it. I can't have this baby.

I can't do that to myself.

It feels worse than cutting, worse than suicide. It feels like a slow form of torture that I'll have to endure until…what? Until I die? What kind of a life is that? Don't I deserve a life too?

I honestly don't know the answer to that. *Do* I deserve a life? What makes my life more deserving than this baby's? The thing is, I can't live my life if I have this baby.

I don't have a choice.

Okay.

I guess I have a choice.

But I can't make *that* choice.

There's adoption. That's what I'll have to do. But I'll still have to tell my parents. I'll still be marked. I'll still have to walk through the school with a big belly for everyone to see. Watch out for the pregnant girl.

I wonder what the rumors will be. *I heard she did it in the gym after school with half the basketball team. I heard it was some guy from her church. I heard she doesn't even know who the father is.* People will make up their own truths, but I would be the only one to really know what happened.

And then one day I won't be pregnant. They'll whisper, *I heard she gave it up for adoption*, and people like my friend Susanna will touch my hand and say, "You gave someone the greatest gift," and I'll smile tightly, like, *Yes, I did. Aren't I just such a saint?*

But somewhere in the back of my mind, I'll wonder. What if Baby turns out to be just like his father?

It can't be helped. Someone will get this baby and it'll be their problem, not mine. I'll have a different problem. I'll spend my life wondering about that child.

Baby is a year old now, I'll think on his birthday, wondering if they bought him a little cake to smash at his birthday party.

Baby's off to kindergarten.

Baby is going to graduate from high school.

I'll look into the eyes of every child I pass who's Baby's age, looking for HIM. God—GOD, IF YOU'RE UP THERE LISTENING—I don't want that life either. I don't want to search every face I see for HIM. I don't want to live my life knowing a piece of HIM and me is out there. It hurts too much… that daily reminder…

But I don't think I have a choice. One of these lives will be mine, and I'll have to live it.

Signed,
Mellie Rivers

February 15
Afternoon
Dear Ms. Tilson,

I'm writing this in the school library. It feels like the only safe place to write anymore. Last night I was writing in the living room since all my siblings were doing their homework at the dining room table, so I exiled myself to the couch. But then Jeremy came in, and peered over my shoulder. "Dear Ms. Tilson?" he read out loud. "Who's Ms. Tilson?"

I slammed the notebook shut. "My English teacher."

"Why are you writing her a letter?"

"I'm not. It's a homework assignment."

"Your homework assignment is to write her a letter?"

"I said it's not a letter!"

"Then why were you starting a homework assignment with 'Dear Ms. Tilson'?"

"I wasn't—it's none of your business, Jeremy!"

He stuck his tongue out at me, like a child. "Jeez, Mellie, what's with the attitude? You on your period?"

I launched myself off the couch. "You are vulgar and disgusting!" I ran upstairs, but Bethany was in our bedroom and kept asking me questions about her homework because I had the same class last year, so I couldn't focus. I wound up finishing my entry from last night after everyone was in bed. And then writing more because I couldn't sleep.

I tried to write in the cafeteria during lunch, but it was stupid of me to pull out the notebook in front of Delia and Susanna. The minute I did, Delia eyed the journal and said, "How much have you written in that? I feel like I am way behind."

And then she reached for it.

I snatched the notebook from her grasp so fast that I knocked over Delia's water bottle. She yelped and grabbed it before it could make a puddle on the table. I shoved the notebook back in my bag, suddenly feeling like I'd come to school naked.

"Jeez, Mellie," Delia said. "I wasn't going to read it. I just wanted to see how many pages you'd done."

"I'm sorry, I—"

"What, have you got some deep dark secret in there?" Delia laughed. "It's not like I don't know all of your secrets anyway."

I forced a smile. My heart was pounding. The notebook felt red hot in my bag at my side. I need to keep it safe. But nowhere is safe.

"I haven't written that much," I said.

"I write every night," Susanna offered. She'd been silent through this whole strange exchange. "Just like a half a page or so."

"It's a stupid assignment," Delia said with a sniff. "I don't see what we're supposed to get out of it."

"I kind of like it," Susanna said. "It's not any different than writing down your prayers."

Delia's eyes narrowed. I could tell that she wanted us all to agree with her, that writing in a journal was some dumb project from a hippy teacher. But I wasn't going to agree with her. I wasn't going to betray what I'd written in my journal like that, not when this notebook is the only friend I have right now.

"Whatever," Delia said. She turned back to me. "Can I borrow your notes on *Hamlet*? I have to retake that test."

"Sure." I dug into my bag. I could feel Delia's eyes on me, on the journal, like she had X-ray vision and could see through its cover to everything inside it. Everything I didn't want her to know.

"Why do you have to retake the test?" Susanna asked.

I handed Delia my English binder and she rolled her eyes. "I didn't do so great on it." Well, you and I both know she bombed the test. I saw the big red D on her paper when you handed them back. But no way was Delia going to admit that out loud. "I was busy all weekend and couldn't study. Ms. Tilson said I could retake it."

"Busy with what?" Susanna asked.

"Wedding stuff." She sat up straighter, her gloaty look that had dimmed with the mention of *Hamlet* back on her face. "We tasted cakes and picked out place settings and floral arrangements. You should've been there, Mellie."

"Well, I was at home studying, which is why I got an A on my test."

"Mel-*lie*," Delia whined. "I really missed you. I thought we were going to do all this together."

"Do what together?" My heart thudded in my chest, like it did now whenever the wedding came up. Once upon a time I would've been *ooh*ing and *aah*ing over cakes and flowers with her. Once upon a time I would've failed my English test too because I was busy helping Hannah with wedding planning all weekend. But now…

"I thought we were going to be helping Hannah plan the wedding together. It was so fun tasting cakes and the baker was this hilarious guy who told the most outrageous jokes—"

"Like what?" Susanna asked.

"I don't remember them now," Delia said, glaring at Susanna. "You had to be there." She turned back to me. "And I really wish you had been." Delia reached across the table and grabbed my hand. "I thought we would have so much fun together, and you're missing all of it."

I looked down at our clasped hands. "I'm sorry," I said. I wanted to be sorry, but I wasn't. The thought of tasting cakes and smelling flowers and pretending to be happy… I shuddered, then pretended to cough so they wouldn't notice. "I was worried about getting all my studying and homework done."

"Well, I think Hannah could use some support. She seemed really on edge. She disagreed with Brandon about everything. It was pretty annoying."

"Really? That doesn't sound like Hannah," Susanna said.

It didn't. Sweet, perfect Hannah, who was going to follow in my mother's footsteps and be a sweet, perfect wife, who doesn't argue with her future husband. "Disagreed about what?"

"Oh, you know, frosting, flowers… He wanted buttercream frosting, she wanted fondant. He wanted lilies, she wanted hydrangeas."

"Well, Hannah loves hydrangeas." But she hates fondant. Why would she dig in her heels about that? I didn't say that out loud, though. "I'm sorry I missed it," I said again. "I'll go next time."

"Good." She squeezed my fingers. "We're almost sisters! It's so exciting!"

"Yeah," I agreed, forcing a smile that felt like a knife to my gut.

I want to be happy and giddy and excited like her. I want to be over the moon that my best friend is going to be my sister by law. But how can I call Delia my best friend when I can't tell her what's happening to me? When I'm so afraid she'll judge me?

What kind of friend is she that I know deep down she would not support me? Even the good memories are twisted now. I wish I could go back to my old life, but it seems so long ago, like looking back through a long tunnel at a place that is slowly fading.

So now the only place that feels like sanctuary during the day is the library, because no one is supposed to talk in there, and if Mrs. Edison catches you looking at anyone's work, she'll lay into you about "keeping your eyes on your own paper."

No one bothers me in the library, no one asks why I'm writing a letter to Ms. Tilson or why I'm doing my assignment at all. The chairs here are really comfortable too, soft and slightly oversized so you can turn sideways and drape your legs over the arm and still have a nice support for your back. Which is how I'm sitting right now. There are about ten other kids, working diligently at the tables or the computers, and probably a couple more in that back corner where everyone likes to make out. I'm pretty sure Mrs. Edison knows about that—how could she not?—but she leaves it alone. I think noise is more offensive to her than kissing.

I keep going back to something Delia said, though, about Hannah being so disagreeable. That doesn't sound like Hannah to someone who knows her like I do. Hannah is sweet and kind and accommodating and *so good* at putting people at ease. But she does have a stubborn streak—a streak her fiancé probably hasn't seen.

Once when I was about nine and Hannah was thirteen, our whole family went camping at this huge cabin in Rocky Mountain National Park. It was a good thing we were in a cabin and not tents, because it rained the whole three days we were there. By evening on the second day we were all totally bored and full of cabin fever. Dad remembered passing a movie theater several miles outside of the park, so we piled into the car. There were two screens. One was showing a newly released horror movie, one of those terrifying haunted-house movies where even the preview makes you jump out of your skin. The other screen was showing an old Disney movie, *The Little Mermaid.*

Of course we were going to see *The Little Mermaid.* Mom and Dad have *never* allowed us to see horror movies. Mainly because a lot of them are rated R and we're not allowed to see R-rated movies. But this particular horror movie was rated PG-13. And Hannah turned to Mom and Dad and said, "I want to see it."

Dad shook his head. "No."

"Why not? I'm thirteen. They're playing at the exact same time. You guys see *The Little Mermaid*, and I'll meet you outside after."

Mom reiterated Dad's answer. "No."

And then, out of nowhere, it became a screaming match. *I'm not a baby anymore. You can't protect me forever. If the Motion*

Picture Association of America says I'm old enough to see it, then I'm old enough to see it. You guys are so unfair. You never let me do anything.

And on and on it went.

Finally, it got to the point where we were going to miss both the movies. Bethany started to cry. Dad bought six tickets (Joanie wasn't born yet) to *The Little Mermaid,* and we left Hannah fuming outside on a bench for the entire length of the movie.

The thing is, Hannah LOVES *The Little Mermaid.* It's her favorite Disney film. I can't tell you how many times I've caught her singing like Ariel in the shower. She would've happily sat through it for the umpteenth time.

The only reason she didn't want to see *The Little Mermaid* was because my parents told her she didn't have a choice.

The mystery to me is, why would she feel that way about her wedding?

I wish I could be there for my sister. I wish I could go to cake tastings and pick out floral arrangements and be happy for her. I wish. I wish. *I wish.*

I want to tell her why I can't, but it will ruin everything for her. I'm not sure that truth is worth it. Even if you destroy one thing to build something better, there is still all that destruction.

I can't put her through that.

At the end of the day, even when she bugs the crap out of me, she's still my sister and I love her. I don't want her to feel pain. Not even my worst enemy deserves that, least of all my sister.

Signed,
Mellie Rivers

February 15
Dear Ms. Tilson—

It weighs on me. This thing I can't tell you. It creeps into my daily life when I'm not suspecting it. Like today at lunch. It was totally normal, just me and Cara and Rowan, having a regular conversation, so regular that I don't even remember what we were talking about. But then:

"*Oh my God*, he's such a fucking hypocrite," Cara said. Rowan and I turned to her. At some point, she'd checked out of our conversation and was scrolling on her phone. I know, I know, phones are strictly forbidden in school, so don't tell on her, okay? She held the phone out for me to see the headline in the *Washington Post*: "President Paid for My Abortion."

It read like a trashy tabloid, but it was not. It was the same newspaper that printed the Pentagon Papers. And there was that headline in black and white; how the staffer who accused the president of coercing her into sex paid for her to have an abortion. To most people, it's probably one more outrageous act in the long string of our president's outrageous acts, but to me it went deeper. That headline was a punch in the gut.

"Can you believe him?" Cara said.

"At this point, I can believe anything," Rowan said.

"I mean, because of him, abortion is illegal in twenty-five states—"

"And because of him, more women are dying," I muttered.

"—and meanwhile he's paying for abortions for the girl he *raped*."

"Well, of course," Rowan said. "Those guys are all against abortions until they actually need one."

Cara's face got very pinched. "*They* don't need one. And who's to say it was that woman's choice? Who's to say he didn't force her to have an abortion? Maybe she wanted to keep the baby, but he wouldn't let her."

"Who would want to keep a baby after they had been raped?" Rowan said.

Cara breathed out hard, like a bull pawing the ground before the charge. "I wouldn't, but the point is, it's *her* decision. Not his. Not anyone's. HERS."

"Yes, I agree—"

"In fact, men shouldn't even be allowed to have an opinion about it." Cara jabbed her finger at Rowan. "No uterus? No opinion."

"What? I can't even say what I think?"

"Nope. Not about this."

"Hang on, that's not fair," Rowan said. "If I was in a relationship with a girl who got pregnant, I'd want her to tell me."

"It's not your choice!" Cara yelled. Lucky the cafeteria was so loud no one noticed. "The minute she tells you, you'll make it all about you—"

"I would not!"

"—because that's what guys do. It's not your fault; it's in your DNA. So suddenly she has to take *your* feelings into account, and she shouldn't have to. She should be able to make that choice without anyone else putting their judgment all over it."

"Wow, Cara." Rowan sat back in his chair and folded his arms. "You have a reeeeaaaallly low opinion of men, don't you?"

"No, I don't. I'm just sick of living in a world that's run by them." She glared at him for a moment, then flicked her gaze to me. I was silent, letting their argument wash over me like an angry wave I didn't want to ride. There is *so much* I wanted to say… I wanted to scream and yell and cry, but I forced it all down. It's like when I'm at the clinic, how I have to remember *Don't engage*, because if I do, I won't be able to stop, and that could be dangerous.

Cara nudged me. "Lise, back me up on this."

I took a deep breath. I thought carefully about what I should say, and then I said only that and nothing more. "I'm sick of it too. Decisions about a woman's body are the woman's choice.

No one else's." I rested my head against Rowan's shoulder. "Sorry, dude."

He twisted in his chair so that I had to sit up again. "You're saying that if you got pregnant, you wouldn't even tell me?"

Cara slapped the table. "Wait a second. Have you guys finally done it?"

"No," we both answered and then faced each other again.

I searched Rowan's face for a long moment. What did he want me to say? "I would tell you," I said at last, "but only after I had decided what I wanted to. And I wouldn't be asking for your permission or advice, I'd tell you I was doing it and that was that."

Rowan bit his lip. "Okay," he said. "That's fair."

The answer I gave him? It's the truth. At least I can be honest with him about that. There are so many important things that have to be left unsaid in this conversation. Why does abortion always come up? Why does it pervade my life? I hate that I can't tell my boyfriend and best friend my most closely held secret. I hate that I can't tell them about all that I've seen.

I *hate* that.

Goodness and trust seem to be finite nowadays. Secrets are used against people and lives are put in jeopardy. I can't risk that. Not for you, Ms. Tilson. Not even for Cara and Rowan. It sucks, not being able to talk freely. The weight is almost too heavy to bear. For as much as I can trust Rowan and Cara, I can't trust that they will keep the secret too. And I don't want them to be burdened with it like I am.

I want to be honest with them, about all of it. Someday, maybe. But not today.

—Lise

February 15
Night
Dear Ms. Tilson,

I've started to think about choices. I guess I really have two options. Keep the baby or give it up for adoption. Those are the only two paths I'd be allowed to take.

But...I know there's a third path. And I've started to think about what would happen if I went down that one instead.

I know I shouldn't. I know I should not think about that third option. That choice is not allowed in my world. Except it keeps popping up into my brain and I keep tamping it down, like a game of Whac-A-Mole that I can't ever win.

If my parents ever found out...they would kill me. Maybe not physically kill me, but their shame would be like dying a thousand deaths. They would probably disown me. It would be like Chava in *Fiddler on the Roof* getting banished for marrying outside the faith. That's how my dad would be. He could not live with me after making a decision that goes against our faith like that.

Still…

Abortion hangs like a forbidden fruit. There's no way I can pick it from the tree.

I wouldn't even know where to go. Okay, that's not true. I know the clinic. Every day, people from my church protest and pray outside of the building, holding up signs that say CHOOSE LIFE. There's no way I could walk through that gauntlet without being seen—without being recognized.

I can't choose *that*.

But I don't know that I can go down those two other paths either.

Signed,
Mellie Rivers

February 16
Dear Ms. Tilson—

I know I'm only sixteen, but sometimes I feel like I should know exactly how my life is supposed to go. We're always told to "think about the future," whether it's SAT prep or considering colleges or other life lessons. Thinking about the future is important, but why can't we concentrate on now?

I have no idea what I want to do with my life, but I feel so much pressure to have a plan. Everywhere I turn, people are talking about college. When I told Mr. Jacobsen at the start of this year that I wanted to organize a Women's Day Fair, the first thing out of his mouth was "Oh, that will look great on a college application." Like that's the only reason to do it. Like I didn't want to have a Women's Day Fair because, you know, it's good and important for the students at our school.

It doesn't help that Rowan and Cara know exactly what they want to do. Rowan wants to be a writer. His plan is to go to

Oberlin for English lit and do his MFA at the Vermont College of Fine Arts. That's, like, the next ten years of his life. I can't even plan this coming weekend. And Cara wants to be a fashion designer and go to FIT. She has a job designing window displays at the mall, and she's already saving her money so she can take an unpaid internship while she's at FIT and still be able to pay for expenses. She's saving for something that's not going to happen for ages. Whenever I have more than a hundred dollars in my bank account, I spend it at Sephora.

But one thing about me: I'm not afraid of failing. If I go down a path and it doesn't work out, that's okay. I'll just start down a different path. If there's one lesson I learned from that stupid school board and trying to change the dress code, it's that I can fail and survive. Not just survive, but get back on my feet with more determination than before. I feel like that's a lesson they don't teach in college, so maybe I'm one step ahead.

I also want to change the world. That seems enormous, like a mountain so high I can't even see its peak. So how am I going to move that mountain? Or really, mountains, because there are so many to be moved. What is it that I want to change most about this world?

Well, that's easy to answer. I want to make things better for women and girls. But there are so many ways to do that. Do I want to be a doctor? Sometimes the answer is yes, but then I think of all those years of school and the heartache I've seen that comes from being a doctor...and I'm not sure that's the right path. Peace Corps? Maybe. How can I effect the most change?

The thing is, I have years to figure this out. I'm only a sophomore. I just wish the world would stop making me feel like I need to figure it out before I've even had a chance to live and decide for myself.

—Lise

February 16
Night
Dear Ms. Tilson,

I'm writing at home because I didn't write at school today. I couldn't get to the library because Mom needed me to watch Joanie after school, so I had to go straight home. Then I had to help Joanie with her reading assignment and play dolls with her and feed her, and it was nonstop. Once again, I could see my life stretched out as one endless *do this with me*, *do that with me*, *I want a snack*, *I'm thirsty*, *I'm bored* if I keep this baby. I can't do it. I'm sixteen. I'm only ten years older than Joanie; I am not ready to be someone's mom.

I think I have to give up the baby for adoption.

Which means I have to tell my parents.

But I'm not ready to do that yet. My palms get clammy and my insides turn hot. I try to imagine that conversation and I can't. It is going to be so awful and I just—

I can't.

Not now.

So instead, I'm curled up in the big squishy chair in the corner of the playroom. Mom is watching that show on TLC about the family with twenty million kids. She *loves* that show, probably because she wishes she had twenty million kids too. Ruth and Joanie are stretched out on the floor. Joanie's wearing her Cinderella dress because she always wears her Cinderella dress after dinner, and Ruth is making a bracelet from her bead kit. Bethany is reading a magazine because it's Friday and she doesn't like to do her weekend homework until Sunday night. Dad is in his study and Jeremy is at an evening class, so it's just us girls. I like it like that. No one is paying attention to me, because I'm in the corner and the TV is loud and everyone is doing their own thing, but we're still together. And I like that too.

The TV show with the twenty million kids ends and the next one comes on. It's about people looking for long-lost family members, and it runs in the background while I write.

It's one of the few shows on TLC that we're allowed to watch, like the show with the twenty million kids. We are definitely not allowed to watch the show about the Amish kids who go wild, or the transgender teenager, which I think Mom even wrote a letter to the network about. But this one is okay, because it's about families finding each other. I glance up as the people on TV start to get emotional. The episode ends with a joyously tearful reunion. Suddenly there's a knot in the pit of my stomach.

This episode—like most—involves an adopted kid who's been looking for his birth mother.

This show isn't just about families finding each other. It's about people who chose not to have abortions.

I sit up. I can't breathe. It's a good thing I'm sitting in the corner, because I'm gulping for air like a hot iron poker is searing my skin. I'm burning, I'm burning, I'm burning...

These people are so happy to find each other.

The mothers always say the same things. *They forced me to give you up*. Or, *I wasn't ready to be a parent. I think about you every day.* And the children say, *it's okay, I don't blame you. I've always wanted to meet you.*

And then the children say, "Tell me about my father."

Tell me about my father.

TELL ME ABOUT MY FATHER.

I try to take slow, deep breaths.

My family is going to see me. They're going to turn around at any second and see me having a panic attack.

The people on the screen are crying, and I can feel my own tears welling in my eyes. *Tell me about my father.* What will I say when Baby comes looking for me in twenty-five years?

Your father raped me on the cold cement floor of my family's basement.

I didn't want to have you, so I gave you up for adoption because the thought of looking at you every day made me sick.

I hate that you exist.

I HATE THAT YOU EXIST.

My whole body is shaking.

Once again, my life stretches out in front of me, one endless day after another, fearing the day when Baby finds me.

I can't.

I can't do this.

No one should ever hear that their mother wishes they didn't exist. I know I can't live with that pain every day. I don't know what I did to deserve that kind of punishment, but it seems excessive even for the most vengeful God.

I can't bring this baby into the world.

Signed,

Mellie Rivers

February 16
Midnight
Dear Ms. Tilson,

Somehow I made it upstairs and got ready for bed without anyone noticing I was having a panic attack. I'd normally think it was crappy that your kid or your sister could have a panic attack without anyone noticing...but this time I'm grateful.

Now it's midnight and Bethany is snoring. I can't sleep. I never sleep anymore. At least I can breathe again.

I've been thinking about my options all night. That third option, the option that isn't an option, keeps surfacing.

Because it *is* an option. I know I said it wasn't an option for me, but...

I hate myself right now. Hate myself for even thinking about it. I'm such a hypocrite. A dirty disgusting hypocrite. Abortion is not okay for other people, but it's okay for me?

My circumstances are different.

How do I know that my circumstances are any different than someone else's? Countless women have been in my exact same situation. I had no idea what making this choice would be like. It's tearing up everything inside me. Before, I sat and judged those other women. Now, I am one of them.

I'm starting to see there is no right decision. It's all so personal, and I don't want anyone judging me for whatever I decide.

But that third option…

IT'S OUT THERE.

And it's the only option that lets me move on.

I just wish I didn't have to make this decision alone.

Signed,

Mellie Rivers

February 18
Night
Dear Ms. Tilson,

I've been thinking all weekend.

There's that scene in *Gone with the Wind* where Rhett comes home from London with Bonnie and there's Scarlett at the top of those great, grand stairs and he says she looks pale and she says it's his fault because she's pregnant and he laughingly says in this careless, callous way that maybe she'll miscarry. She gets so mad at him that she strikes out at him with her fists and he smoothly steps out of the way and down those great, grand stairs she falls and sure enough, she miscarries.

One in four pregnancies end in miscarriage. I learned that from Mom after her miscarriages.

Signed,
Mellie Rivers

February 19
Dear Ms. Tilson—

The weirdest thing happened during gym class today. Mellie Rivers threw herself off the balance beam. I don't mean she fell, I mean, she *threw herself off it*. She didn't think anyone was watching, but I saw it. Why would she do that? That's weird, right?

I followed her out of the locker room into the girls' bathroom, the one way down by the gym that no one ever uses except to get high. (In case you didn't know—people get high in that bathroom. But you didn't hear it from me.) When I went in, I found her in the end stall, crying. She cried the whole period. THE WHOLE PERIOD. I sat next to her. (It was my lunch period, so I wasn't skipping.) Have you ever sat next to someone while she cries for an hour? It tears your guts out. I thought my heart would break from listening to her. I wanted to say something profound and helpful, as if I could make all that pain go away in one sentence. All I actually did was give her my compact to fix her face afterward. I didn't know what else to do. I felt so helpless, and I *hate* that feeling.

You're probably wondering: "Who is Mellie Rivers to you? Why would you waste an hour of studying to sit with some random girl while she cried?" Let me tell you a little bit about Mellie and me. We have a history. We used to be friends. Like, ten years ago. We were really good friends, actually. We were in the same Girl Scout troop. We sang about making new friends and keeping the old. We exchanged friendship bracelets. We went to movies together. I remember having movie night at my house and watching *Charlotte's Web*. We both cried at the end. We were those kind of friends.

Then Stella Jacobs-Meyer joined our troop. Stella has two dads. (Who are both freaking awesome, by the way. Her dad Tom makes the best spaghetti Bolognese I've ever had, and that includes in a restaurant.) It was back before the Supreme Court took its head out of its ass and legalized gay marriage, and Mellie's family had a *big* problem with the Jacobs-Meyer family. They probably still do.

Anyway, Mellie's parents yanked her out of our troop. She was going to Country Christian at the time, and I didn't see her again until she came to public school in ninth grade. I thought we'd be friends again, because we had some really fun times when we were kids. But she had a different social circle, and, well, it just wasn't going to work out. Which is fine. I'm very happy with my own group of friends.

But something pushed me to follow her into that bathroom this afternoon. All I could think about while I was sitting there (ceramic tile is really cold BTW, especially when you're wearing a skirt) was why she would launch herself off the balance beam and then cry for an hour? And if she has such a close circle of friends, why wasn't one of them with her?

Something is up with her. Maybe it's not my place to worry—no. That's not true. It *is* my place. Even though we don't hang out anymore, I never stopped being her friend. And you never give up on your friends, no matter how far apart you've drifted.

—Lise

February 19
Afternoon
Dear Ms. Tilson,

I used to be able to talk to God. I don't mean like Joan of Arc and her voices. I used to be able to go to a quiet place and tell Him my secrets. I always felt like He was listening. No matter what I told Him, He was listening.

Now I guess I have to settle for you and this journal.

He's gone. I can't feel Him anywhere anymore.

I used to feel Him everywhere, even at school. Today I was alone in the girls' bathroom by the gym (the one no one uses except to get high—you know about that, right?) and I thought I might feel Him there. That He'd hear me crying all by myself and comfort me. Nope. Instead, I got Lise Grant.

Lise Grant is a poor substitute for God, in case you were wondering.

She must've followed me into the bathroom. I was in the

last stall when I heard the door open. Then, *click-clack*, *click-clack*. I peeked underneath the stall door. *Click-clack*. Two feet appeared clad in black pumps that had two bright red lips printed across the toes. I recognized those shoes. This morning Bethany pointed at them on our way into school and said something mean like Lise Grant might as well go sell herself on a corner in Pinecrest if she was going to dress like that. I held my breath. Maybe Lise didn't know anyone else was in the bathroom. Maybe she'd come in to get high. I bet Lise Grant gets high.

But those bright red lips were pointed in my direction. Lise was standing in front of my stall. A second later there was a knock on the metal door. "Mellie? Are you okay?"

How did she know it was me? More importantly, why did she care? I haven't talked to Lise Grant in ten years. I swallowed, forcing the sobs out of my throat before I spoke. "I'm fine. Thank you."

Her obnoxious shoes didn't move. "Are you sure? I...I saw you fall in gym."

"That was an accident. I'm fine."

"Okay." One shoe lifted and then set back down. "Only...it didn't look like an accident."

"Why would I throw myself off the balance beam on purpose?" My voice sounded high and sharp, like the lady doth protest too much.

"I don't know. There could be a million reasons. I just wanted to make sure you were okay."

I told her I wanted to be alone, but she wouldn't leave. She claimed it was her lunch period and she didn't have to be anywhere. I had study hall, but Mr. Wright would assume I was at the library because I pretty much have a standing library pass. As soon as she left, I wanted to get back to crying, to not talking to God some more.

Instead of leaving, those stupid black-and-red pumps stepped closer to my stall. And then, Lise Grant slid down onto the floor, her back against the wall, the two of us separated only by the dented, pink metal door.

Why would she do that? It's none of her business why I was crying in the bathroom. Her hand rested on the floor, right between the door and the floor, hovering on the border between her space and my space. Like she was reaching out. Like she was chiseling a door in the wall between us.

"I really want to be alone," I told her. It would've been more effective if my voice hadn't cracked on the word "alone."

My whole life I had never wanted to be alone. I had always wanted to be in the circle of my family, surrounded by people and by God. I'd never had the need to be alone. I've never had to listen to my own thoughts without anyone else's crowding in. Now that was all I wanted, and Lise Grant wouldn't give it to me. *Lise Grant*, of all people.

Lise didn't say anything. She also didn't move. Fine. If she wanted to sit there while I cried, then fine. It's a free country. I lowered my head back onto my knees and gave in to the sobbing. For the rest of the period, Lise sat against the wall with me, listening to me cry. When the bell rang again, I dug the heels of my hands into my eye sockets, stood up, and opened the door. "I don't know what that accomplished," I said.

Lise slid up the wall until she was eye level with me. "Sometimes when we think we want to be alone, we really need someone to just be there for us," she answered.

I tightened my jaw and brushed past her to the sink. My reflection in the mirror was a mess. I splashed some cold water on my face. When I straightened, Lise was holding out a powder compact to me. "Here," she said. "It'll cover up the splotchiness."

"Gee, thanks."

"Hey, I've cried in the bathroom more than my share. I'm prepared."

But see, Lise Grant is the type of person I'd expect to find crying in the bathroom. Lise Grant probably has her heart broken by a different boy every month and gets into fights with her friends. She needs to be prepared.

I took the compact and dabbed the powder all over my face. It did help. "Thanks," I said and handed it back to her.

She dropped it into her bag. She was watching me in the mirror. Then she said to me, "Look, Mellie, I know you have no reason to confide in me, but you can talk to me. I know how to keep a secret."

Why would she assume I was keeping a secret? I mean, if I don't want to talk about it, that means I DON'T WANT TO TALK ABOUT IT. Why is that so hard to understand?

She followed me all the way to biology. Well, okay, she's in the same class, so she had to go that way anyway. But the whole time, she was just like, "I get it if you don't want to talk, but if you do, I will listen."

Finally, when we were outside the classroom, I asked her, "Why? We haven't been friends for ten years. Why on earth would you want to be my friend now?"

Lise looked at me, like she was searching my face for an answer to a question she hadn't asked yet. She stared so long that I noticed how the flecks of gold in her green eyes make her whole face light up like there's a perpetual ray of sunshine above her. "Just because we haven't spoken in ten years doesn't mean I stopped being your friend," she said. "I was always your friend, whether you wanted me there or not."

She and I sit on opposite sides of the biology room, but all through class I could feel her presence like she was sitting right beside me. In the same way she'd sat beside me the whole previous period, filling my silence with her presence.

Then, after school, she caught me on the stairs on my way outside and gave me her number. She said, "I know you think all sorts of things about me, but the truth is, I'm a decent person. And you can talk to me. If you need to."

The piece of paper with her number on it gleamed in the fluorescent light, like the handle of a pot I know is too hot to touch. "I have people I can talk to."

Lise tucked the paper into my coat pocket. "I'm pretty sure that if that were true," she said, "you wouldn't have been crying alone in the bathroom."

And then she just disappeared like a ghost. She was off to go hang out with whoever she hangs out and do whatever she does after school. It's like she just popped in to drop a bomb and then poofed away before she had to deal with any of the aftermath. She told me she thinks I'm keeping a secret, but doesn't stick around to hear what it is. Who does that?

Not that I would've told her anyway.

So far, you're the only one I've told.

Signed,
Mellie Rivers

February 19
Midnight
Dear Ms. Tilson,

I almost did it. I almost told my parents tonight.

Almost.

So close.

THISCLOSE.

The words “I’m pregnant” were on the tip of my tongue, on the verge of spilling out.

Everything out in the open.

I wanted that relief. No more secrets.

I was sitting at the dining room table, my homework spread out in front of me, and Dad leaned over my shoulder to peer at my algebra homework. “This one,” he said, pointing. He gave me a wink. “Is that your final answer?”

“No,” I whispered. I erased what was there, thought for a second, and put in the correct answer.

"Smart girl," he said with a smile and sat down across from me to read his paper.

Mom came in and kissed the top of my head as she walked past me. I suddenly remembered all the nights she has done this, all the kisses: on my forehead at bedtime, on my knees when I skinned them, on my cheek at church. *Peace be with you. And also with you.*

I had this vision in my mind that if I told them, they would hug me tight and tell me it was going to be okay. That whatever I decided, they would support me.

My heart—it hurts—I can't breathe.

We were alone in the dining room after dinner and I thought: Tell them. Tell them now.

I wanted my vision to be true so bad that it strained my heart, like a muscle stretching too far.

I wanted to tell them. No. That's not true. I wanted—I want—that alternate version of my family. The one where they support me no matter what I decide.

The words were about to spill out of my mouth when there was a knock on the door. I heard Bethany open it and then HIS voice was in my living room. HE was here, in our house. My whole body started to shake. The pencil fell out of my fingers. But my parents…they didn't notice. Dad got up to greet our guest with one of those guy-hugs, the kind where they clap each other on the back, and Mom got this delighted smile on her face and followed my dad. They left me, trembling like an earthquake, in the dining room.

I can't tell my parents what happened. They are not my imaginary family. I can't expect them to be different people, and my secret will shatter this house to its core.

They would side with HIM. Their standing in this town, this state, is so tied up with his. I would be a problem who needed a solution.

My chest is tight just thinking about it now. Bethany is asleep, and I'm in the closet with the door shut writing by the glow of a small flashlight trying to breathe again, as if the safety of this enclosed space will expand my lungs.

There's something comforting about the complete darkness in this closet. It's warm and smells faintly of mothballs from a generation past. The cotton and wool of my clothes surround me, and my toe grazes the butter-soft leather of my ballet flats, waiting to be worn in summer.

Nestled in here, I know the truth. I can't trust my parents with this secret. I wish I could. But I can't tell them. I have to figure out how to get through this some other way.

I tried yesterday. Falling off the balance beam in gym class wasn't an accident. But it didn't work. It wasn't like in *Gone with the Wind*, where one careless comment from Rhett and a spill down the stairs gets rid of a baby.

I don't know what to do.

I think I need help. I have to tell someone. Not my parents. Someone else.

But who?

Signed,
Mellie Rivers

February 20
Morning
Dear Ms. Tilson,

I spent the whole night in the closet. I crept out just before dawn, before Bethany woke up and asked what I was doing curled up on the floor. I thought about that, about what I would say if Bethany found me. Could I tell her? Except Bethany's younger than me, too young to help. Even though she says our parents can be lame, Bethany also craves their approval. Like the rest of us. Like I used to. So I got into bed silently in the near-dawn, knowing that I can't trust her with this.

Downstairs, after breakfast, Hannah cornered me at the sink. "Can you taste cakes with me this afternoon? I'll pick you up at school."

I turned on the water and began to do the dishes. "I thought you did that already."

"I picked out the flowers. I didn't settle on a cake."

"I have homework," I said, scrubbing scrambled-egg residue off the spatula.

"Come on, Mellie. You promised you were going to help me with the wedding when I got engaged, and you haven't helped at all."

Guilt gnawed at my stomach. I glanced at her as she twisted the engagement ring on her finger. When she first got engaged, she showed off that ring like it was the baby Jesus himself on her finger. I used to think it was pretty, but now I think it's obnoxious. Is it possible to have too many diamonds? The ring is huge—too big for Hannah's slender fingers—and not at all elegant. It screams, "Behold! I am taken!"

"Will it only be you and me?"

"Yes." Hannah nudged my arm. "Just come. How often do you get to eat free cake all afternoon?"

I snorted, but kept my face turned away. I put the last dish in the dishwasher and closed it. "Okay," I said. "I'll go."

At least it will only be the two of us. But I'm dreading that too. It's so hard to hide my feelings from Hannah. She's known me since before I knew myself. I'm afraid to be alone with her, afraid I'm going to spill...afraid eating all that cake is going to make me sick.

I wish I could be honest with her. Of anyone in my family, she would be the one to hug me, tell me it would be okay, and that she'd support me whatever I decide. But the thought of telling her makes my skin go hot and fills me with shame.

I have to go to school now. I'll write more tonight.

***

Cake tasting wasn't awful. It was actually kinda great. And a little weird. Because something is up with Hannah, but I don't know what it is.

When I got in the car in front of the school, she was on the phone with her fiancé. The only reason Hannah has her own cell phone is because he bought it for her. Mom and Dad wouldn't have allowed it otherwise.

"I'm at the school now," she said, waving to me as I ducked into the passenger seat. "I have to go. Why do you need me to call you from the bakery?" Silence. I couldn't hear what was being said on the other end. Hannah chewed at her lip. "No, I…I know how to pick out a cake we'll both like." More silence. I could hear his voice rising through the phone, but couldn't make out what he was saying.

"Fine. I said fine. No, of course I'm not mad. I'll call you from the bakery. Uh-huh. Me too." She glanced at me briefly as she set the phone down and pulled away from the curb. I didn't say anything.

"That other bakery we went to had the worst buttercream," Hannah said as we drove. "And the baker fawned all over Brandon, who ate it up with a spoon. The fawning *and* the buttercream."

"She flirted with him? That seems inappropriate."

"No—it was a man! And he wasn't gay." Hannah turned the

car onto a narrow side street and pulled alongside a pretty building painted robin's-egg blue. "The florist was gay, but he had the good sense not to flirt with my fiancé. No, this guy assumed Brandon would be making all the decisions, so he flattered him up and down, ignoring me. It was rude."

"Um, doesn't the bride usually make all the decisions? What was that guy thinking?"

Hannah turned off the car. She stared out the across the dashboard, breathing a long sigh. "You know Brandon. He walked in there, all big man on campus, and I was the little woman who nodded along with him."

I studied her profile. It wasn't like Hannah to question, deride, mildly insult the man she was about to marry. She'd been groomed to be the perfectly agreeable wife...much the way I have. And Bethany has. And all of our father's daughters have. Was she starting to buck the tradition?

"Is the flavor of your wedding cake that important to him?" I asked, thinking about the phone conversation I'd just overheard.

Her shoulders tensed slightly. Then she turned to me, a bright smile across her face. "Everything about the wedding is important to him. Come on, let's go in."

I could feel the falseness behind that bright smile. I followed her out of the car and into the bakery, which was charming. The baker was a very smiley lady who kept bringing us cake after cake after cake to taste. And *oh, were they good*. White chocolate raspberry. Red velvet. Dark chocolate with chocolate cherry ganache filling. Vanilla with blueberry buttercream filling. I stuffed myself rotten. And I didn't get sick.

In fact, eating all that sugar made me feel good. Actually happy. Was there some magical ingredient in cake that makes you forget your problems as long as you are shoveling forkfuls of chocolate mousse into your mouth?

While we were tasting, Hannah and I laughed over stuff we haven't laughed about in a really long time. "Remember the time Mom told me to make fresh lemonade for one of Dad's mayoral campaign rallies, and I forgot to put in the sugar?" Hannah said after we'd finished off the slice of white chocolate raspberry.

"Yes! And everyone still drank it!"

"Because they were too polite to say anything!"

We cackled like two mischievous hens. The baker brought over another slice—vanilla cake with a dark chocolate butter-cream frosting—and smiled at us. "Now, that's what I like to see," she said. "A bride who knows how to enjoy herself."

Hannah smiled back at her, but it was the same overbright smile she'd given me in the car. I watched her take a forkful of the cake before digging in myself. Was she genuinely enjoying herself? We were having fun, but she froze up at the mention of the wedding. Why? This match is what everyone wants. The Rivers family and the Talbot family are close friends. Of course their children should marry. They'd been courting forever...

high school sweethearts. So what was going on? Why wasn't she over the moon? Where was the rosy glow that all brides are supposed to have? I haven't seen it…I can't remember ever seeing it.

"Weren't you supposed to call him from the bakery?" I asked after our seventh piece of cake.

"This is my favorite," Hannah said, pointing her fork at vanilla cake with dark chocolate frosting. She sighed and licked the last bit of frosting off her fork. "Yeah, I guess I should call." She pulled out her phone. When she turned on the screen, I could see it was filled with texts and missed calls. The top one, the most recent, was in all caps. *WHERE R U? WHY AREN'T U ANSWERING UR PHONE?*

I sucked in my breath hard and fast. Hannah glanced at me. "He's just stressed out," she said. She sent a quick text back—I couldn't read it—and clicked off the screen. She pointed at our empty plate. "I wish I could get this one."

"Why can't you?"

"Brandon would never approve of a cake without white frosting. He's so traditional. Like Daddy." She rolled her eyes. "Can you imagine Daddy's face if his eldest daughter had a cake frosted in chocolate? Oh, the shame!" Then, she got this little gleam in her eye, the same gleam she got before the *Little Mermaid*/horror movie incident.

I leaned forward. "Don't tell him. What's he going to do? Prevent the cake from being served at the wedding?"

Hannah's lip curled into a tiny half smile. "Which one? Brandon or Daddy?"

"Is there a difference?" I asked with a snort before I could stop myself. I gasped. "I didn't mean—"

"No, you're right." Hannah's jaw tightened. She barked out a short, sharp laugh that didn't sound like she was amused at all and waved her hand toward her phone. "I'm marrying my father. What a fucking cliché."

Ms. Tilson, I have never ever heard Hannah swear. In fact, this could've been the first time in her whole entire life that she swore. I was so taken aback that I couldn't speak. There were so many things I wanted to say, to ask her, to confess, to spill my secret at her feet, and I was just about to open my mouth when—

"Well? Did you decide?" The baker was back, her dimpled smile kind and encouraging. "Is the vanilla with dark chocolate buttercream *the one*?"

Hannah took a deep breath. "Is it possible to do a dark chocolate cake with a vanilla buttercream frosting? A white cake will go better with our color scheme."

"Absolutely," the baker said. "Now that we have the flavor, let's talk design."

And that was it. Hannah was back to being the perfect wife who nodded along, a pretty white cake to match her pretty white life. I sat by numbly while she called her fiancé, apologizing before she'd even said hello. I said nothing while he berated her so loudly that I could hear him too. I stayed quiet when he calmed down and Hannah put him on speaker with the baker. He dominated the discussion of roses versus lilies and the ratio of fresh flowers to edible sugared ones, making the final decision, despite what Hannah wanted.

But I saw it. Her streak of rebellion, that inner life that is brighter than all the muted colors she's forced into. What does it mean? I don't know. But once she marries him, it's over. She's done. She can't walk away from that life, not in our world, not without losing everything.

It hits me—neither can I.

But no matter what I decide, in some ways, I've already walked away.

Signed,
Mellie Rivers

February 21
Dear Ms. Tilson,

I saw you today at the Women's Day Fair, after school in the gym. I'm starting to really hate the gym. It smells like sweat and dirty socks and failure. That is not conducive to morning sickness. It was a miracle I didn't throw up.

You probably saw our table and rolled your eyes. Most people do. Despite the banner that took me two weeks to create and the fresh flowers that Delia brought, no one was crowding around to read our pamphlets on keeping yourself pure until marriage. I mean, let's face it. Most kids aren't too interested in staying virgins. And the ones that are already know what's in our pamphlets. So our table wasn't exactly popular.

When Delia and I signed up to have a table at the Fair, I was still a virgin. I still thought I had total control over that decision. I had no idea that choice would be taken from me.

Sitting next to me behind our pretty, flower-covered table,

Delia made a snort of derision. I followed her gaze to the RAINN table, where everyone seemed to gravitate. Probably not because they were victims of rape or incest, but because Cara Sullivan sat on the edge of the table in a very short skirt, holding court. My jaw clenched. How dare she? How dare she sit there, chatting happily, surrounded by pamphlets about what to do and who to call if you've been raped? As if she had any clue what it was like to be raped. To be violated. To be carrying the baby of your violator, a constant reminder of your failure to remain pure.

Red-hot anger surged through me. I grabbed my water bottle and unscrewed the cap with shaking fingers. Gulping down water, I tried to cool the anger in my veins. It wasn't her fault that she didn't have a clue about what it was really like to be raped. It was my fault that I did.

"Hey, did I tell you my mom's blog hit five hundred thousand?"

I turned to Delia. "What?"

"My mom's blog. It hit five hundred thousand followers the other day."

"Oh, really? That's great." I reached out to straighten the pamphlets on our table. We got them from church, so they were a little cheesy. Not that I'd tell Delia that. Her mom designed them. She did all the newsletters and pamphlets for the church.

I picked up one, a glossy trifold that read *God & You: A Very Special Relationship* in black cursive across the front. The background was pink with flowers around the border. Inside were several paragraphs about how God wants us to save ourselves for marriage, that the bond between husband and wife is as sacred as the bond between a person and God. The brochure was clever. It never specifically stated "this applies only to girls" but that was implied in every detail.

My fingers tightened on the pamphlet, wrinkling the edge. A few months ago, I never would've noticed that. I never would've been aware of the subtext. It's like my blinders have been removed.

But I'm not sure I like what I can now see.

"Yeah, she might get a book deal," Delia said.

"Wow." I glanced around the gym, only half listening. The Equal Pay for Equal Work table was giving away free donuts.

"Yeah, my dad just wants to make sure it's not going to take up too much of her time before she signs anything. He doesn't want her to have to travel or anything."

I nodded and moved around the side of the table. It was hard for me to look at Delia these days. She picked up a stack of *Make the Promise: Save Yourself* pamphlets (also pink, also floral) that advertised the purity ring sales, and began tapping them on the table too. Years ago, Delia and I had made that promise in our church youth group. We put on those little gold rings, a sign of our vow to stay virgins until marriage. I looked down at my hand. I still wore my ring, a burning brand on my finger that seemed to scream "Liar! Liar!" every time it glinted in the light. But I couldn't take it off. That small action would be noticed, and I'd have to give a reason. I tucked my hand behind my back and looked out over the array of pamphlets on our table.

"How come there aren't any pamphlets for boys?" I asked before I could stop myself.

Delia stopped tapping her stack of papers and laid them squarely on the table. "Um, because this is the Women's Day Fair?"

"Yes, but..." I swallowed. "Shouldn't we be teaching guys how to treat women too? Shouldn't we encourage them to make the same promises that we make?"

"Well, sure, but...you know." Delia rolled her eyes. "It's not the same for boys."

"It should be."

"But it's not."

I pressed my lips together and sucked in my cheeks. Had I always been as blindly accepting as Delia?

Delia's gaze returned to the RAINN table. "Did you see what Cara Sullivan is wearing today? She's such a slut."

It didn't escape me that Delia had changed the subject. She always deflects when something makes her uncomfortable. I totally get it, Ms. Tilson. I really do. If it hadn't been for what happened to me, I probably wouldn't be questioning the pamphlets either. But now I can't help it. I see questions in everything I used to think was true beyond reason.

"Oh…yeah," I said weakly, hoping if I was noncommittal enough, Delia would change the subject again.

"I can't believe her parents let her out of the house looking like that."

"Mmmm." I glanced at the clock to see how much time was left.

"You know, I heard she's done it with at least three guys."

I sucked in a breath. "That's not really our business, is it?"

Delia arched an eyebrow at me. She doesn't like it when I call her out. She pinched her lips together and looked back at Cara. "Someday she's going to go on one of those spring break trips and be raped and left for dead on a beach."

"Delia." My voice came out so sharp that Delia leaned away from me. "Don't joke about that."

"I wasn't joking. I was stating a probability." Her lip curled. "Lighten up."

My red-hot anger was back, pulsing inside my chest. "Don't ever, *ever* joke about rape. It's not funny."

Delia stared at me for a moment before holding up her hands. "Okay, okay. Cheese Louise. Calm down."

My jaw clenched so tight my teeth scraped against each other. In that instant, Ms. Tilson, I hated Delia. I hated her stupid "Cheese Louise" expression, I hated her mom and her mom's sanctimonious pamphlets, and I hated her for being so judgmental about people she didn't know. If she knew, if she only knew…then what? What would she say about me if she knew the truth?

She would stop speaking to me. She would call me a liar, a fraud, a sinner, and then she would walk away. Our friendship was based on what we had in common, and anything outside of those boundaries would destroy it.

I took another swig of my water. The nausea was back. Delia leaned against the table. "What's with you lately? You've been really moody and, like, dark."

Moody and dark, huh? I could feel the angry confession bubbling at my lips, like a pot threatening to boil over. Part of me didn't care about destroying our friendship. I just wanted it out there. I sucked in a breath and held it. This wasn't the way to do it. Not here, not now, not in the middle of the crowded gym where anyone could overhear and where Delia wouldn't hesitate to make a scene. "I'm just stressed."

Delia gave me a sympathetic look. "The wedding? I'm sure Hannah is wigging out over every last detail."

I forced a half laugh that came out like a snort. "Hannah and my mom are superstressed." This wasn't true, but it was an easy lie. "I guess it must be rubbing off on me. Sorry if I've been a pill."

Been a pill? Since when did I say things like that? That was something my mother would say. I wrapped my arms around my stomach. Wasn't there a pill you could take to get rid of a baby?

You probably needed a prescription…and I couldn't exactly go to my pediatrician. What was I thinking? Could I actually do what I was considering doing?

"Hey, Delia," I said before I could change my mind. "Do you think there's ever a case when having an abortion is okay?"

Delia's eyes widened. "Where the heck is that question coming from?"

I shrugged, trying to look casual. "I was thinking about what you said about Cara. What if someone was raped, and they got pregnant? Do you think abortion is justifiable in that situation?"

"No," Delia said, her voice flat and firm. "It's never justifiable."

My insides felt hot and itchy, like I was wearing them on the outside of my body.

Delia tossed her head, flinging her long braid over her shoulder. "Don't punish the child for the sin of the father, right? You could always place the baby for adoption if you don't want to keep it."

I knew that she was saying *you* like it was anyone in the world, but it felt as if she was slapping me across the face. "But… she'd still have to carry the baby, go through nine months of constant reminders of what happened…and what if it was incest or something? Or what if something was wrong with the kid?"

"Every baby is a blessing from God," Delia said in a singsong voice, and I swear at that moment I could see the sanctimonious light shining from her face. I wanted to punch that light right out of existence. I don't think this baby is blessing. Maybe someone else in my situation would, but I definitely don't. And maybe someone else would make a different choice, but it's her body. This is my body, and no one has the right to tell me what to do with it.

Holy crap.

This is my body, and no one has the right to tell me what to do with it.

Did I just write that?

Am I…pro-choice?

Okay, you're probably sitting there reading this like, *Well, duh.* And maybe I have been all along. But in my family, in my circle, you're just…*not.* People from our church sit outside the Whole Women's Health Clinic almost every day, reading from the Bible as women go in and out. My dad talks about closing down that clinic as part of his campaign platform. That clinic and every other clinic that perform abortions in Colorado. He talks about making abortion illegal here like it is in so many other states. And my mom…

My mom had one.

It's family lore. How she was going down a dark path and my dad's love saved her. How not having that baby is her biggest regret. She's given speeches at pro-life rallies about it. Paraded out onto the stage next to my dad as an example of "Abortion Regret."

You can't be pro-choice in my family. It's pro-life or bust.

But it's now starting to hit me how hypocritical that term is. *Pro-life*. There is only one life they are pro, and it's not mine.

Signed,

Mellie Rivers

February 21
Dear Ms. Tilson—

Jason Bellows is an asshole. Do you have him in any of your classes? If you do, I'm sorry. He's the worst. He probably sits there the whole time making doodles of girls' breasts. He is a walking definition of toxic masculinity. He thinks he's God's gift to women, when in fact, he's a curse. A black magic, helter-skelter curse.

I can't believe I dated him two years ago. UGH. Seriously, just writing that makes me embarrassed. What was I thinking? I guess I can chalk it up to being fourteen and an idiot. Thank God we never did anything major, physically. Just some over-the-clothes stuff. He wanted more. That's pretty much why I broke up with him. *He kept talking about it.* Like, every conversation we had would turn to sex. Who was doing it, who wasn't doing it, why weren't we doing it, and when would we do it? One weekend his parents went out of town, and I knew he was expecting it to happen. AS IF.

I'm pretty sure if I had ever been alone with him, and said no, he would've forced me.

It makes me wonder if there are girls at school who he did force. The thought makes me sick.

Anyway, backing up, today was the Women's Day Fair! The culmination of my hard work. Okay, it wasn't that hard. I got people to sign up to host tables, and I got the maintenance staff to set up the tables. But still—it was *my* idea! It was the first time a Women's Day Fair has ever been held at Wolverton High, and even if it wasn't on the actual Women's Day because of scheduling, I did this. I made this happen. I'm not too modest to say I'm proud of that.

Cara and I hosted the RAINN table. We got a pretty steady stream of people. Most of them came to chat with us, but we did get some people who were interested in Rape, Abuse & Incest National Network. I mean, you hope it hasn't happened to people you know, and it's not like someone is going to necessarily walk up and talk about being raped. Although, we did have one girl who did do that! I'm not going to say who. But she was pretty open about it. I thought that was really brave. She was mainly interested in RAINN because she wants to volunteer when she's older, share her experience so she can help others. Which is awesome.

I want to be the kind of person who volunteers and helps people. Maybe our table helped some people today, but one table at one event seems really insignificant. Especially because it wasn't the table I wanted to host. That would have been too dangerous. I can't even tell you why, because as open as I want to be in these pages, I can't be open about that. Besides, the school probably wouldn't have let me.

Anyway, the reason I bring up Jason Bellows is because he pulled Delia Talbot's braid in front of my table. True, who hasn't wanted to pull that stupid-looking braid of hers to see if it would wipe that smug look off her face. But he did it because he's an ASSHOLE, and he thinks he has the right to put his hands on a girl's body whenever and wherever he wants. He's disgusting. Delia tried to pull away from him, and he snapped her braid like it was reins on a horse. I was out of my chair in a flash to push him off her, and he tells me, "Go back to your RAPE TABLE"—as if that's an acceptable thing to say—so I knocked him and his dumb, hipster messenger bag on the floor.

Luckily, no teachers saw me, and Jason isn't going to report that he got knocked down by a girl. Because you know what would've happened if a teacher had seen me? I would've been the one hauled into the principal's office. Not Jason. It's infuriating, and part of the double standard that made me protest the dress code.

I think if you had seen the whole incident, you might've sided with me. But you'd be one of the only teachers. Women need to stand up for each other. We get enough shit from guys. It pisses me off when I see girls putting each other down. There are so many good things we could do with that energy.

That's why I stood up for Delia. She didn't even say thank you, just walked off in a huff. But I didn't do it for a thank-you. I would've been there for any girl.

Okay, so maybe part of me did it because I'm still mortified that I dated Bellows. But it was like 80 percent for the women of the world.

There's one more thing I want to record here tonight. Remember how I told you I think something is going on with Mellie Rivers? I'm almost sure of it, and now I might have an idea what it is.

She took a pamphlet from my table. *What to Do If You've Been Raped.*

Was that why she was crying in the bathroom?

Are the two things connected?

What if they are? I can't be sure. Picking up a pamphlet doesn't prove anything. And it's not my business. Not unless she talks to me, which she clearly doesn't want to. But...I get the sense she's not talking to *anyone*. She and Delia are best friends, but they seemed to have gotten into an argument at the end of the fair. When I saw Mellie afterward, I told her she could talk to me, anytime.

Why is this so important to me? Why do I keep pushing her to talk to me?

I can't answer that, Ms. Tilson. My gut says I can help her, and that I have to keep trying.

I'll end on that dramatic note.

Your Favorite Drama
Queen and Do-Gooder

—Lise

February 21
Later
Dear Ms. Tilson,

I never told you about the rest of the Women's Day Fair, and there was more to tell. I got distracted by the revelation that I'm pro-choice. Remember how I said I see questions in everything now? That's one thing I never would've questioned. Because I never thought I would need to. I was never going to be in a position where I would need an abortion. All those mistakes that women make were going to happen to someone else. But I didn't make any mistakes; I did everything right, and now here I am.

Delia left me alone at the table to explore the fair. It was a relief not to have her there. I watched her saunter through the crowd, her long braid swinging down her back. She disappeared behind a cluster of seniors, kids I didn't know. I looked around. There were so many kids in this gymnasium who I didn't know, who I've never bothered to know. Were any of them going through the same thing as me?

A shriek echoed off the gym walls, and the seniors scattered. Jason Bellows had grabbed Delia's braid, tugging so hard her neck jerked back. My skin turned icy, breath frozen in my lungs. Him touching her like that, his hands on her like he had a right to her body—

"Let go, Jason," Delia said. She was pissed, maybe even panicked—or maybe the panic was mine. I gripped my chair, wanting to get up to help her, but I couldn't make myself move.

"Giddyup, horsey!" Jason laughed, slapping Delia's braid up and down like a harness.

"Let go!" she shrieked, her neck and face flushed.

He laughed harder. "Shouldn't be wearing reins if you don't want to be bridled. Whoa, girl!"

That laughter—it broke me. I bolted from my chair. But before I reached Delia and Jason, Lise Grant slammed him in the side, knocking him away from Delia. "What the hell is your problem, Grant?" he shouted.

"My problem is you harassing her," Lise said, facing off with Jason. She planted her hands on her hips. "You don't touch a girl without her consent, and you stop touching her when she tells you to stop."

"Whatever. Go back to your rape table."

I gasped, but Lise never missed a beat. Before I could blink,

Jason was on the floor, the contents of his messenger bag spilled next to him. His buddies clustered around him, laughing and pointing, while he turned a deep shade of red. Lise leaned over him. "Next time I'll kick you in the balls." Then she turned on her heel.

Lise grabbed a bottle of water from her table and handed it to Delia. "You okay?"

"I'm fine," Delia snapped. "He was just teasing me; it was no big deal." She pushed the water bottle away and stalked across the room.

What the hell is wrong with Delia? Lise stood up for her—something Delia had failed to do for herself—and Delia hadn't even thanked her. I know we haven't exactly been friends with Lise, but is Delia so judgmental she couldn't even accept a kindness? And Jason's behavior wasn't teasing. It wasn't "no big deal." I now saw it for what it was—dangerous.

I watched Lise in conversation with Cara, who sat in another chair behind their table. The two of them were throwing dark looks at Jason, who was collecting everything that had fallen out of his bag. Lise didn't agree with anything Delia believed, but she still defended her.

This is what I had to come back to write in my journal, Ms. Tilson. Delia is the daughter of our church's pastor, but Lise acted way more Christian than her today.

It made me think. What type of person do I want to be

friends with? And maybe more importantly, what kind of person do I want to be?

"Hey, Grant, I think you broke my fountain pen," Jason called out.

"Hey, Bellows, I think you're a sexist pig," Lise called back. Cara burst out laughing. The two of them leaned into each other, talking trash about Jason in overly loud whispers, their attention turned away from the table. I sidled by, mixing in with a couple of other kids who were passing at the same time, and swiped a brochure. *What to Do If You've Been Raped.* It was light blue with dark gray block lettering. No pink or floral for RAINN. I tucked it into the pocket of my cardigan, hoping no one had seen me take it.

At the end of the fair, I threw all of our church pamphlets into the plastic storage bin, but before I could close it up, Delia snatched it away from me. "What is your problem, Mellie?"

I stared at her, my stomach all twisty. "What do you mean?"

"Last year you were in the middle of the gym, forcing those pamphlets into every student's hand who passed. We didn't have any left." She slammed the lid on the bin. "This year you could barely be bothered to get off your butt. It's like you don't care anymore."

Heat flamed in my cheeks. "I didn't see you in the middle of the gym either, handing them out," I retorted.

"Well, I'm not the president of the club," Delia snapped. "And I'm not the one moping around and being a bad friend."

"*I'm* a bad friend?" I reached forward and yanked the bin out of her arms. "I'll take this back to the church. Don't do me any favors."

"Cheese Louise," Delia yelled. People turned to look. "I don't know what is wrong with you, but I really don't want to be around you until you figure it out." She stomped out of the gym without once looking back, her braid swinging behind her.

I blinked, the corners of my eyes stinging. She's right, of course—there *is* something wrong with me. She's not the problem—I am. Hot shame snaked through my gut, leaving a roiling wave of nausea in its wake. I hurried toward the locker rooms as fast as that damn bin would allow me and slammed into the first stall. Everything I'd been holding in all afternoon came up in one rush. I vomited until my throat was sore. When I was sure my stomach was empty, I staggered out of the stall and rinsed my mouth at the sink. My tongue tasted rancid. I need to start carrying a toothbrush with me.

I picked up the bin and stumbled through the halls to the front doors of the school. I was almost there when a shadow fell into my path. "Hey."

"Jeez!" The bin fell out of my arms and cracked open, the pamphlets spilling out in all their pink-and-floral glory on the floor. "Okay, you have got to stop sneaking up on me."

"I'm sorry." Lise squatted on the floor and began to gather up the pamphlets. "I didn't mean to scare you."

"Well, you did a good job of it." I lowered myself to her level, trying to move slow so the nausea didn't come back. "How did things go at your table?"

"Okay, I guess." Lise tossed a handful of the latest church newsletters into the bin. "Except for that idiot Jason Bellows."

"Yeah." I shivered. "Thanks for—what you did. For Delia."

Lise shrugged. "Girls gotta stand up for each other." She held up the *Make the Promise: Save Yourself* pamphlet and shook her head as she tossed it into the bin. "I'm sorry, I just can't get behind that abstinence-only stuff."

I grabbed a stack of the pamphlets away from her. "Nobody's asking you to get behind it."

"I'm sorry, I just—you know, studies have definitively proven that comprehensive sex education is the best way to prevent teen pregnancy and STIs."

Hearing that word on her lips, just thrown out there so casually like I was a statistic, something bubbled over inside me. "We're not talking about preventing pregnancy or STIs. We're talking about making a commitment and sticking to it. About respecting yourself enough to wait." I bit down on my lip to shut myself up, because I could feel the tears coming. I would've stuck to that commitment if I'd been allowed to.

"Okay," she said. "I can get on board with that reasoning. But you can respect yourself and still have sex before marriage too, you know." She shrugged. "I just don't think it's for me. I mean, I wouldn't buy a car without taking it for a test drive, would you?"

I glared at her. "That is a disgusting analogy." I threw the last few pamphlets in the bin and snapped the lid on. "You're talking about the sacred bond between two people, not a car."

"But you can be in love—real, true, sacred love—without being married," Lise said. "Look at Goldie Hawn and Kurt Russell."

I rolled my eyes at her. "Are you serious? That's the best you can come up with?"

"Eva Mendes and Ryan Gosling?" Lise suggested.

"Ryan Gosling?"

"Come on, you gotta give me Eva and Ryan. Ryan, Mellie." She fluttered her eyelashes. "*Ryan*."

I looked at Lise. A smile spread across her mouth and she started to laugh, crinkling her eyes up at the edges. I snorted again. I couldn't exactly bring myself to laugh but the sound, the feel of her laughter lightened something inside me. "Okay," I said, "I'll give you Ryan Gosling."

"Anyway, sorry for scaring you." She lifted the bin off the floor and held it out to me.

I took its weight into my arms. It felt heavier than it should, full of shame and doubt and broken promises. "Thanks." I opened the door with my back, sweeping cold air and the smell of snow into the hallway. The sky was gray and cloudy, limning the world in shadow. I started down the steps.

"I saw you take that pamphlet."

Lise's voice, quiet but firm, made me turn. The chilly air swirled around me. "What pamphlet?"

"The RAINN one." Lise stepped down one stair so that she was just one above me, our eyes almost equal. "I saw you put it in your pocket."

"No… I—" I swallowed. My whole body went hot and cold all at once, from the inside out. I couldn't scramble up a lie fast enough, none that were believable. "It's not for me."

Lise raised an eyebrow. "Really?"

"Yes. It's for—the church. The secretary was saying the other day they wanted to have more crisis resources. So I grabbed one to show her. In case they want to have them at the church too." God, it sounded so stupid, then, as I said it and, now, as I write it down. An excuse so paper-thin that she had to see right through it. It actually seems impossible that no one else has seen it when it feels so obvious to me.

But after an eternally long moment, Lise just lifted a shoulder. "Okay," she said, dropping it in a shrug. "If you say so." She jogged down a few steps, but before she reached the bottom she turned back to me again. "But if that's not the truth—if it wasn't for, you know, the church…" She took a deep breath, and I could feel the weight in her next words, how she measured them with care. "You can talk to me, Mellie. I mean it. I'm here."

She left it at that and hurried up the sidewalk, her head bent against the wind. I just stood there and watched her go. She gave me one last wave as she turned the corner. I watched her for a long time after she disappeared, unable to move.

One minute or a lifetime later, it started to snow.

Signed,
Mellie Rivers

February 22
Dear Ms. Tilson,

I'm writing this during my prayer circle meeting. I'm writing this during my prayer circle meeting because no one but me is here. I got here early, so it wasn't weird at first. Three minutes turned to five, then ten... Finally I got up and walked out into the hall and down to the big picture window that looks out over the front steps of the school. Sure enough, there was Delia with Susanna and all the rest of my friends, walking away from the school, presumably to have their own prayer circle somewhere else, without me. I feel like Delia saw me at the window, but I can't be sure. I've always known she has this vindictive streak, but it's never been directed at me before.

I wish I could say I don't care, but it hurts my heart, like a pulled muscle that won't heal. All those years of friendship, of shared secrets and memories, were a lie. She wasn't ever my friend, not really, not if she can't be my friend when it counts the most. If she was really my friend, she wouldn't write me off so easily. And honestly, I wish I were still living in the blissful ignorance of our fake friendship. I wish I didn't have this *thing* I can't tell her and we could just go on the way we've always gone on, even if it is a lie.

At least it's quiet in this empty classroom.

It's easier to piece out my thoughts in this kind of quiet.

I know you think I'm a hypocrite. I am.

All these years, I never thought abortion was okay. But now it's *me* and it's okay. That is the textbook definition of hypocrisy.

Here's the thing. It wasn't me before. Meaning, I believed what my family told me I should believe. I didn't really think about how I felt about the issue myself, if I were to put myself in someone else's shoes. I didn't know what it was like to actually walk in these shoes. And now I have them on, and they're too tight and uncomfortable and they rub on my heel and I've got blisters all over my toes. I get it now. This isn't a situation anyone would ever choose to be in. You just find yourself in it, and then you have to make all sorts of horrible decisions in order to get yourself out.

I used to think abortion was a black-and-white issue. If you had one, you were a bad person. If you chose not to, you were good. Except there are a thousand shades of gray in between those two extremes. I get it now that I'm one of those shades.

My mom is one of those shades too. I always put her in the

good camp because she's my mother. You don't really want to think about your mom being a bad person. But now I realize—she's not good or bad. She's just human.

In all those speeches she gives, my mom talks about how much she regrets her abortion. How she wonders who that child would've been, how she counts how old she/he might've been, how she prays every day for forgiveness for the choice she made. But now, I'm replaying her speeches in my head, and I'm hearing what she *doesn't* say. How if she had kept that baby, she never would've married my dad. She doesn't talk about how she lives in a nice, big house with a husband who supports her so she can stay at home with her six children—all of whom she probably wouldn't have had if she'd kept that baby. Everything she has, she has because she didn't have that baby.

But that's never the way it's been presented. Instead, it's all about her regret over one baby.

I was ten years old when my youngest sister was born, and I remember it well. Joanie was born at home, so I was there when she came into this world. It was such a happy occasion, especially because it was easy. Having already had five kids, my mom's body had gotten good at the process. When Joanie came out, she was laid on my mother's chest, and she got this smile on her face. "What a blessing," she said. I assume she said it after each of us. Because we were all blessings. Every baby is a blessing. That's what I always thought. How would I think any different, seeing how incredibly happy my mom was bringing my sisters into the world? I've never known a baby who wasn't wanted, a cherished addition to their family.

Maybe that's why it's always been so easy for me to accept that every baby, no matter how he or she was conceived, is a blessing.

Every baby. Every baby. *Every baby.* I've heard all the speeches about it in my dad's campaigns, at the pro-life rallies my mom has taken me to. It's been drilled into me, ingrained in the fiber of my brain.

Have you ever tried to change something that is so fundamental to your being? It hurts. Like physically hurts. Right now, that change and that pain is all beneath the surface, invisible to anyone but me.

Pretty soon, the reason for all this change will become clear to everyone. My jeans already feel too tight. I had to sew in an elastic to close them and make sure my sweater covers the zipper even when I raise my arms in the air.

I don't have a lot of time left before everyone can see, and all that pain will be visible on the outside.

Signed,
Mellie Rivers

February 22
Dear Ms. Tilson—

Rowan and I almost had sex today.

This afternoon he came over, because our moms were both at work, so of course we made out on the couch. We would've done it, except neither of us had a condom, and we were not going to risk it. After he left, I started to doubt what I felt when we were together. Did I really want to have sex with him? Am I ready for that?

First of all, I want to make clear that he's not pressuring me in any way. Rowan is a good guy. His mother is a granola hippie who's been talking to him about consent since he was two. So that's not the issue. He's not the issue.

Then what *is* the issue? Is there one, or am I just overthinking it because that's what I do? The thing is, in the moment, on the couch, I wasn't thinking at all. I was lost in him, lost in how good it felt, lost in how happy I was. It was only when we stopped that I started to think.

Sometimes I think I should think less. See how bad I am? I have to think about not thinking. I guess what I mean to say is, I should do more, jump in faster, be spontaneous.

Because the truth is, if there had been a condom, I would've done it. Without thinking too much.

So I've made up my mind. I should just do it, right? Right. Right? I guess the next time I'm at the drugstore I should buy some condoms.

—Lise

February 22
Night
Dear Ms. Tilson—

Okay, my mind is not made up. I'm all twisted and I can't sleep. I'm lying here awake in the middle of the night, listening to the creak of the house and the wind outside. Maybe it's excitement, you know, nervous anticipation about making the decision to finally do it. Except…I don't think that's it.

This afternoon, on the couch, I thought I knew what I wanted. I mean, hands everywhere, clothes half off, my skin so warm wherever it touched his… It was good. Going further would probably feel even better. Why wouldn't it? Rowan loves me. At least, I think he does. He's never said it. But he does stuff, like leave me a Snickers bar inside my locker before seventh period because he knows I need a little afternoon sugar to get through biology. He calls when he says he's going to call. He helped his mom make homemade veggie noodle soup when I had the flu and brought it over, then sat on the couch and watched about seven hours of *Gilmore Girls* with me. *GILMORE GIRLS*, Ms. Tilson. That's gotta be love.

But he's never said the words.

Neither have I.

The thing is, I'm not sure I love him. I mean, I love him. I love him in the way a girl loves a guy for sitting through seven hours of *Gilmore Girls*. But I'm not sure I love him, like buy-a-plane-ticket-and-run-through-an-airport-to-give-him-one-last-kiss-at-the-gate kind of love. That gotta-have-him-now kind of love. That can't-live-without-him kind of love.

Then again, maybe I'm asking for too much. Maybe that love is just in movies. I mean, I know all about this Cinderella fantasy that society has created for women. My mom says the best kind of love, the best kind of marriage, is built on friendship. Partnership. Gee, Mom, thanks for making marriage sound like the most unromantic thing ever.

But maybe in the long run, growing old together on a foundation of mutual respect and understanding *is* the most romantic thing ever.

UGH. Do you see why I'm so twisted up about this?

Do I lose my virginity to someone I'm not sure I love, but I know cares about me and respects me, or do I hold out for an elusive ideal that may never come?

I guess I always imagined I'd lose my virginity to someone

who I wanted to spend the rest of my life with. Even if we break up a month later, at the moment we have sex, I want to believe we're going to be together forever. That he is *the one*, the love of my life. But if it turns out that he *isn't the one*, does that make the fact that we slept together better or worse? Will it break my heart?

If I have sex with Rowan, I don't think I'd be risking my heart. I think...if we broke up...my heart would be okay.

I know it may sound weird, but maybe I should lose my virginity to someone who has the power to break my heart.

And I'm not even getting into all the risks of pregnancy, STIs... So what's my rush? I know plenty of girls who are still virgins. Well, three. No—wait—two. Jesus. Only two of my friends are still virgins? So again I ask—what is the rush? Why does it feel like girls are expected to lose their virginity in high school?

I don't want to be a statistic.

I wish there was some magical sign that would tell me what the right decision is. Some neon billboard flashing DO IT or WAIT.

What would Lorelai Gilmore do?

Wait. Lorelai Gilmore got pregnant at sixteen.

Bad example.

—Lise

February 23
Night (back in the closet)
Dear Ms. Tilson,

I don't get Hannah anymore. I just don't. Three days ago we were laughing over old times while eating cake. Today she's a different version of herself, one I've never seen before, smug and self-righteous. She's already acting like those perfect wives at our church, their smiles wide and bright while they whisper behind each other's backs. Where is the old Hannah, who used to make fun of them? I want to smack this smugness off her face. She acts like she understands the secrets of the universe because someone proposed to her. Like she's got it all figured out. Well, I have news for her. She doesn't have a clue. Not one teeny tiny inkling of a clue.

Tonight during dinner, she turns to me and asks in front of the whole family, "How come you're not talking to Delia anymore? What did you do to her?" Everyone at the table stopped, forks in midair, and stared at me. Delia and I have been best friends since forever, and if we're not speaking, they assume it has to be something I did. Because Delia is the daughter of our pastor and that makes her golden. Spotless. Untouchable.

Also, me and Delia not talking? That *just* happened. Like, two days ago. And Hannah knows about it already? Delia must've told her brother, who told Hannah. All within the last two days. Like a game of telephone.

I looked around the table at my family, their eyes all on me like firebrands, and swallowed the chicken that was still in my mouth. It stuck to my throat. "I didn't do anything," I said. "She stopped talking to *me*."

"She must've had a reason," Mom said.

I didn't even look at her. Of course she would take Delia's side. I can't rely on her to protect me like the Mama Bear she used to be. She won't stick her neck out for me. Not if it means risking Dad's reputation.

"I have no idea," I said to Hannah, instead of answering Mom. "We hosted the Girls for Christ table at the Women's Day Fair on Wednesday, and after that she stopped talking to me."

"She said she didn't think you pulled your weight," Hannah said.

No wonder Delia told her family we weren't speaking. She wanted to throw me under the bus before I threw her under it.

"Okay, so if you already knew why she was mad at me, why did you ask me?"

"Mellie," Dad's voice boomed, making me jump. "I don't like your tone."

"I don't understand why Hannah is bringing this up," I said, slamming my fork down. "It's between me and Delia. It's none of your business."

"I can't have my maid of honor fighting with one of my bridesmaids," Hannah said. More like whined. Like the Hannah that I tasted cakes with a few days ago has left the building. "Fix it before you ruin my wedding."

"OH MY GOD!" Then it was my voice that made everyone jump. "That's all you care about! Your stupid wedding! You don't even care that I got dumped by my best friend."

"Mellie!" This time it was Mom.

I stood. "May I be excused?"

"Actually, young lady, you can go to your room and think about your attitude. I'll call you when it's time to clean up. Which you will be doing by yourself."

"Fine." I stomped upstairs. But by the time I reached the second floor, the chicken had risen up to my throat. I barely made it to the toilet.

As I sat on the cold bathroom floor, I wanted to hate Hannah. What is wrong with her? One day she's the old Hannah, and the next day she's the soon-to-be Mrs. Talbot. I don't get it. If she were awful all the time, I could write her off in my mind and not care anymore.

But then I think about what she's marrying into, and I feel pity.

Pity and fear.

Signed,

Mellie Rivers

February 24
Night (after a looooong day)
Dear Ms. Tilson,

I wish I were eighteen. You know why? So I could *not* vote for my father. I would get an insane amount of pleasure in that. Walking into that booth and checking off someone else's name on the ballot.

I'm still shaking, so I'm sorry if this entry is hard to read. Today was like one of those horror movies where the main characters can't see what's really going on until it's too late. Where everything seems to happen in slow motion until suddenly there's a man with an axe right outside your window and you have no way out.

Today I finally saw the man with the axe.

This morning at breakfast my mom asked me how much homework I had this weekend. Right then, my hackles should've gone up. I should've said that I had a ton of homework and no free time. But instead, I told the truth; I finished most of it in study hall yesterday.

"Great!" Mom said. "Your dad has a rally in Woodview and really needs our support."

I shot Bethany a look across the kitchen table. She gave a small shake of her head that clearly said, *don't even try to get out of it.* I guess she already tried and failed.

"Wear a skirt," Mom called to us as Bethany and I climbed the stairs after breakfast. "Something long so your legs are covered."

In other words, look like the good conservative girls we're supposed to be.

My wardrobe has no shortage of long skirts and dresses, because I've never been allowed to wear a short skirt or jeans to any of my dad's rallies. After all his campaigns, they've piled up. The problem is that most of them are too tight on me now. I had to dig deep into the back of the closet to find one with an elastic waist, and then I covered it with my nice long tunic sweater, which has always been a bit baggy.

When I emerged from the bathroom, Bethany raised an eyebrow. "You're wearing *that*?" She was dressed in one of her best dresses that made her look cool and elegant. "How old is that skirt?"

"I want to be comfortable," I said, which wasn't a lie. "You know how long we're going to be on our feet. Besides, my coat will cover most of it." This winter, Mom bought us all new coats because she knew we'd be on the trail with Dad. I really love my coat. She let us choose our own, and I picked a trench-style wool coat in a deep brown and red plaid. It wasn't cheap, but Mom didn't balk. Probably because she knew I'd be on display. She doesn't skimp when she knows other people are watching.

That's how at 9:30 on a Saturday morning, I found myself in our SUV with the rest of my family, on the road to Woodview. Hannah got out of it because she's "dealing with wedding stuff." For a moment, I almost envied her.

But the rest of us were there to rally for my dad. On the car ride to Woodview, Jeremy went on and on about how he's been stumping for Dad all over campus. He goes to Mountainview Community College. Bethany and I had to hold back from rolling our eyes, because Mom kept turning in her seat to lavish praise on him. Sometimes it is truly disturbing how much she dotes on him.

Even though it was about twenty-eight degrees, the rally was outside on a makeshift stage in the middle of the town square. Dad likes outdoor rallies because people who are walking by tend to stop and listen, so it basically has to be a blizzard of catastrophic proportions for him to hold a rally indoors. My family and I stood off to the side while the mayor of Woodview introduced Dad. I looked around the square. Woodview is different than Wolverton, a little more run-down, a little more rustic.

There were a lot more people in cowboy boots and hats here, more pickup trucks than SUVs. Dad loves these kinds of towns, where the population is a little more working-class than at home. He thinks they're easier to influence.

When the mayor called Dad onto the stage, we all followed him up the rickety stairs. Dad took his place at the podium, and we fell into line behind him, Mom in the middle so she was just behind his shoulder. She positioned herself like that so when someone takes a picture, they can see Dad and his dutiful wife, with their children surrounding them.

I looked out into the crowd, which was smaller than most rallies we've been to, probably because no one wanted to stand out in the cold. Everyone was shivering. In the front row, the press corps looked like their hands were frozen around their recording devices. I felt bad for them, because they *had* to be here.

"The moral fiber of this country is shredding. It is up to us to weave it back together..."

I've heard this speech so many times since Dad announced his candidacy for state senate last year that I have it memorized. It's seventeen minutes long, and it touches on most of the election's issues. The "moral fiber" theme runs through the whole thing in subtle and not-so-subtle ways. There's the section about how crime has gone up since marijuana was legalized, about the attacks on religious freedom (though he really only means Christianity, rather than all religions), and how gay marriage is threatening the traditional values we've always held dear.

My dad is an amazing public speaker. His voice rises and falls like a symphony. He's filled with passion as he talks about these issues. It is easy to understand why everyone nodded and clapped, the word *yes* rippling through the crowd as he underscored his points. I agree with him on some things. I don't think marijuana should be legal, mainly because now that kids have easier access to it, they're coming to school high. And they're driving high. The number of accidents caused by impaired driving has increased since legalization.

But most of the stuff? It's backward. Like gay marriage. The Supreme Court said banning it is unconstitutional. Move on. How about we focus on solving homelessness or the fact that probably half the kids in Woodview don't get enough to eat? These are issues my dad doesn't talk about. It is more important to him that the "moral fiber" of this country be mended than people have food and shelter.

Then he launched into abortion. He saves it for the end of his speech because that's the note he wants to end on. "We all have work to do. Our mission is to show the country that we want to protect life and we want to improve it. Those in need don't need a handout; they need our hands, helping them be a part of a vibrant community that sees the potential in every human being."

I mean, you really gotta admire how he eases into it, how

he couches it in caring for families. A lot of people nodded and "*mmm-hmm*ed" along with Dad. I also noticed some people shifting uncomfortably. A few even walked away, shaking their heads. This seems to be the issue where a lot of people draw the line. Almost everyone who walked away or looked uncomfortable was female. I used to get angry with people who walked out in the middle of his speech, but now I understand it better. Now I'm not sure I'd want a man standing on a platform telling me what I can't do with my body, either.

"I envision a country where families are strong and where women have real choices. And we're already turning this vision into reality, with crisis pregnancy centers across the state."

Dad paused. This was usually where he wraps up, but instead, he took a breath and gave a portion of the speech I've never heard before.

"As you know, there are very few clinics remaining in Colorado. It's been a source of shame that one of those clinics is in my hometown. Every day I have to drive past it and think about the babies who are murdered there. About all the lives ruined there, because every woman who has an abortion has to live with the regret of what she's done."

Mom shifted from one foot to the other.

Dad's gaze swept over the crowd. "As your state senator, it will be my priority to follow the lead of so many other states and make Colorado an abortion-free state. A state where all of us, including our women and children, can live healthy, happy lives. A vote for me is a vote for that future. Thank you, my friends."

He reached back and grasped Mom's hand, pulling her forward so they were standing side by side, arms raised in victory. The show was over.

Except we couldn't leave yet. The press stood up, all their hands in the air, wanting to ask questions. My dad pointed to one and then another. I don't even remember their questions. My mind was still swirling about his declaration to make Colorado an abortion-free state. What does that even *mean*? How could that be possible? He could outlaw every abortion clinic in the state, but could he make every pregnancy wanted and celebrated?

As the questions wound down, my dad pointed to the one female journalist in the press pool.

"You say that you want an abortion-free state for the health and safety of women. What about cases like Lanie Jacobs? An abortion would've saved her life, but the hospital refused to perform the procedure and, as a result, both she and her baby died. Do you think there needs to be exceptions for cases like that? Or in the case of rape or incest?"

My breath stopped in my throat. The Lanie Jacobs case was all over the news. I'm sure you've heard of it. The only comment I heard from my parents when it was in the papers was, "Oh, that poor man." Meaning Lanie's husband. Nothing about the woman who actually died.

I think I expected my dad to say yes, there should be exceptions. That the mother's life was just as valuable.

I think, in that moment, I still loved my dad.

He leaned into his microphone. "What happened to Lanie was tragic and unfortunate. The hospital was put into an impossible situation. Under the circumstances, they made the right decision. Performing the abortion was against their policy, and there was no guarantee that an abortion would've saved Lanie."

Extreme cold flooded me from inside my heart. Did he really believe this? Did he really value women so little? Everything went blurry around me and all I could hear was the sound of my own inability to breathe. My dad's voice pierced through.

"As for cases of rape and incest," he went on, "I believe that attacking a child because of its father's mistakes is wrong. Besides, it's extremely difficult, if not impossible, for a woman to become pregnant through rape. Making exceptions would create loopholes that any woman wanting an abortion would find her way through."

Suddenly I wasn't cold anymore. I was hot, so hot. I was a flame, turning my father's words into ashes and cinders. *I was red-hot living proof that he was wrong.* I was a flesh-and-blood example that yes, you can in fact get pregnant from rape.

I looked over at Mom. She had that placid stand-by-your-man look on her face. Ruth and Joanie were by her side. I hoped they were too young to really know what Dad was talking about. To understand its direct implications on their own lives. Jeremy—I couldn't even look at Jeremy. He's a mini-Dad.

My gaze slid to Bethany. Her eyes were downcast, her expression closed off. Like there was a lot going on inside her brain, but she refused to show it. I furrowed my brow. Did she disagree with Dad? Did she think the same things I did?

Once again, I wondered if I could tell her. If I could trust her. But I don't think I can risk it. I stepped back a little so that there was a space between me and the rest of my family. I was separate. No matter what choice I make now, I'll always be different.

I wanted to run fast and far. To someplace where I would not be judged or yelled at or told what to do. Someplace where I could think my own thoughts. Someplace safe where I could make this choice *for myself*.

If I tell my parents, they will make me keep the baby. I don't know that I'm prepared to do that.

If I tell Bethany, she'll always look at me differently.

If I tell Hannah, she'll never be able to look at me again.

This journal is the only safe place I have.

Signed,
Mellie Rivers

February 26
Dear Ms. Tilson—

I have to confess something. I've been stalking Mellie Rivers since the Women's Day Fair last week. I mean, not really stalking, just keeping an eye on her during school hours. I can't stop watching her. Remember when I said that I never stopped being her friend? Well, I didn't, and a good friend knows when something is up. And something is up with her.

She used to eat lunch with Delia Talbot, but now she eats alone in the cafeteria annex with all the loners. Meanwhile, Delia eats with their other friends in the main part of the cafeteria.

(Note to self: Invite Mellie to sit with me at lunch tomorrow.)

She also goes to the bathroom after every period. I haven't gone so far as to follow her in there, but I'm dying to know what she's doing. Crying? Puking? Is she bulimic? Maybe she just drinks a lot of water? She carries a water bottle with her, and

I see her refilling it at the water fountain at least twice a day. So maybe she's just peeing a lot?

(Note to self: I need to hydrate more.)

Mellie goes to the school library after classes are over. I do too, but I've been going to the library after school since freshman year. Mellie's not a regular. Now she comes every day. She doesn't seem to be working on a project. I walked past her yesterday—casually, totally low-key—and she was writing in her journal. This journal; the one for your class.

A little while later, her sister Bethany came in and as soon as Mellie saw her, she slammed her journal closed and pulled out her textbooks. Bethany asked if she was going home soon, and Mellie said she had a bunch of research to do for an English paper. Maybe it was true, but it seemed like she's avoiding going home.

I've also noticed that her prayer circle has disbanded. They used to meet every Thursday afternoon—the same time as my Amnesty International group. But last week as I was going to my meeting, I saw Delia and the other girls leaving school together. I have to pass the classroom where they usually meet, and when I glanced in, Mellie was sitting there all alone. Why did her friends run out on her? What could she have possibly done to them? Mellie is a genuinely nice person. I can't imagine her pissing off five girls simultaneously. I think this is fallout from their argument after the Women's Day Fair, and Delia dragged their other friends with her. Delia seems like the type of girl who would do that.

Then yesterday Mellie made a phone call from the pay phone down the street from school. Maybe she doesn't have a cell phone, but why wouldn't she use her home phone? Because she doesn't want to be overheard, that's why.

Those are the facts I've gathered, but here's an observation: Mellie just seems—lonelier. Grayer. She's always had a bright aura and now it seems dimmed. It's as if a light inside her has gone out.

All these things taken separately might be nothing, but together they add up to something.

You're probably reading this and thinking, *Why, Lise? Why does this matter to you so much? Why are you getting so emotionally involved in something that has nothing to do with you?*

I'm asking myself the same questions and I can't answer them. I don't know why I feel pulled into this, why I feel like this is my business when it really isn't. But until I know Mellie is okay, I'm not going to stop.

—Lise

February 26
Dear Ms. Tilson,

I called the RAINN hotline today. I waited until after school, when the street was empty except for a few stragglers and the afternoon was fading into dusk. I used the pay phone at the end of the block. It's lucky there still is a pay phone, because I can't exactly call from my home phone.

Someone answered after the first ring. "RAINN hotline, this is Lucy. How can I help?"

I hung up.

Lucy can't help me.

No one can.

Signed,
Mellie Rivers

February 27
Dear Ms. Tilson—

Tonight Rowan took me out to dinner for our one-year anniversary. One year! It feels like longer. I've known him all my life, so it seems like we've been together forever. He took me to that fancy new steakhouse over in Mountainside Plaza. He wore a suit and I wore a pretty dress, and it was like we were playing at being grown-up. Except without alcohol. Everyone around us was much older and drinking a lot of wine, while we had iced tea with our steaks. He held my hand across the table as we waited for our food, and we talked and talked and talked. That's the best thing about Rowan. I can talk to him for hours and never feel bored.

He knows me so well that it's actually a little scary. The only other person who knows me like that is Mom. So he knows when something is bugging me.

Before dessert came (chocolate molten lava cake—so

freaking good) he said, "There's something on your mind lately, isn't there? Do you want to talk about it?"

The thing is, if I had said, "No, I do not want to talk about it," that would've been okay. He never pushes. He listens. He'll offer advice or help if you ask, but he won't try to fix your problem without permission.

"There is something, but it's weird and you're going to think I'm a freak."

"I already think you're a freak," Rowan said, laughing. "So, you know, no danger there."

"Ha, ha." I looked out the window. It's really pretty up there at Mountainside, and the moonlight was hitting the mountains just right. "You know Mellie Rivers?"

"One of the mayor's daughters? Yeah."

"I don't know." I shook my head. "I used to be friends with her, like forever ago. But I still care about her for some reason—"

Rowan interrupted me. "Not for some reason. You care about her because that's who you are. That's your nature."

I tilted my head to the side. "Thanks. But I feel like something is going on with her."

"Going on how?"

"I don't know. It could be nothing. It's probably nothing. But I can't shake it. It's like this gnawing feeling in my gut. I'm worried about her." I bit my lip. "I followed her the other day," I admitted. "Like, around school. I'm insane, Rowan."

He smiled. "You're not insane. This is what you do."

"Stalk people around school?"

He rolled his eyes. "No, you care about people. You don't give up on them. You're like an emotional detective. You don't give up until you get to the heart of the matter."

"An 'emotional detective'?" I grinned. "I like that."

The waiter came with our dessert and we were silent for a few minutes while we dug in. The cake made us speechless. It was that good. But after a few bites, Rowan put down his fork. "Look, whatever is or isn't going on with Mellie, follow your gut. We both know you're going to find out or die trying. I'm just glad you told me. You've been distracted and I was worried it was something I'd done."

Then he picked up his fork, scooped a bite of cake onto it, and held it across the table for me to eat. I leaned forward and took the bite, my gaze on his. My insides were as molten as the lava inside the cake. He pulled the fork out of my mouth and the words tumbled out with it, as easy and familiar as our relationship has been. "I love you, Rowan."

His eyes lit up. "I love you too, Lise."

I slid out of my chair and went to him, kissed him hard. His arm snaked around my waist and he held me tight against his side. I didn't care if everyone in the restaurant was staring. I was just so happy those words were finally out there. I pulled away slowly, and we finished our cake. We still have not had sex. And that's okay.

I do love Rowan. I do. Am I going to marry him and spend the rest of my life with him? Probably not. But if we did, at least I know I'd spend a lot of my life being loved.

—Lise

February 27
Evening
Dear Ms. Tilson,

There's a billboard as you drive into Wolverton. I'm sure you've seen it. PREGNANT? WE CAN HELP. There's a picture of a worried-looking woman (white, pretty, young) holding a pregnancy test with two pink stripes clearly visible on it. Below is a 1–800 number and the words YOU HAVE OPTIONS.

I called that number today. I called from the same pay phone I used to call the RAINN hotline. This time I didn't hang up.

It was so cold there on the corner, the little booth around the phone no match for the wind. A woman's voice answered, "Pregnancy Counseling Center." Her voice was nice. Warm. Reassuring.

"Hello," I whispered into the phone.

"Hello," she replied. "How can I help you, dear?"

It was the "dear" that got me. I hunched over the receiver. "I—I'm pregnant, and I don't know what to do."

"That's why we're here," the woman on the other end said. "We're here to help. You called the right place. When was the date of your last period?"

I forced the words out through my numb lips. "I—I don't know. December, maybe. A couple of weeks before Christmas."

"Have you taken a pregnancy test?"

"Yes. It...it was positive."

"Well, the first step would be to come in so we can give you an ultrasound and see if the pregnancy is viable."

My stomach dropped. "I... That might be hard."

There was a pause. Then, very delicately, like her voice was fragile glass, she asked, "How old are you, dear?"

"Sixteen."

"Do your parents know?"

I shook my head, then remembered she couldn't see me. "No," I said quietly.

"That's okay, dear. They don't need to know. We'll take care of you. Can you come in tomorrow afternoon? After school?"

Tomorrow. I could tell Bethany and my parents I was working in the library again. I'd have to get to the clinic without being seen, but if I went after the school crowd thinned out, I could probably slip over there.

"I can get there," I told the woman.

"Good. Can I have your name, dear?"

My name. I hadn't thought this far. If she had my name, she

would know who I was. Everyone knows the Rivers family, by name if not by sight. "It's…Melanie." I'd been called Mellie for so long that most people didn't know my given name. But what if someone at the center knew me when I got there tomorrow?

"Do you have a last name, Melanie?"

"It's confidential, right? If I come see you?"

"Of course, Melanie. Everything between us is confidential. We'll sec you tomorrow."

I was silent.

After a pause, the woman continued, "It's all going to be all right, Melanie. We're going to take care of you."

I put the receiver gently back into its cradle. Tomorrow. Tomorrow I'll have answers. Tomorrow I won't have to carry this alone.

Signed,

Mellie Rivers

February 28
Dear Ms. Tilson—

I followed Mellie after school today. I overheard her tell her sister she was going to the library and she'd be home by dinner. But she didn't go to the library. I was going to catch up to her and say hi, try to get her to talk to me, but she breezed right past the library. I hung back to see where she was going (into another classroom, maybe? The guidance counselor's office?), but she went all the way to the front door. There she stopped, looked around to make sure no one was watching, and left. Apparently my stalker skills have improved considerably, because she didn't notice me.

I waited at the top of the steps until she had turned right at the corner. Then I followed her across town, hanging half a block behind her. Occasionally she peered around, like she was worried someone might see her. But she didn't see me.

The route she took, the direction she walked…I know well. But I couldn't quite believe it. Not Mellie Rivers.

Except she didn't go where I thought.

She went across the street.

She went to the pregnancy center that's run by anti-choice organizations. The people at that clinic trick girls into going there by saying they're going to help them, then they tell them lies about what will happen to them if they have an abortion. Like they'll get breast cancer. You don't freaking get breast cancer from having an abortion.

Half the staff of these places aren't trained medical professionals. And some of the clinics aren't even licensed. The clinics deliberately set up offices across the street from legit women's health care centers to confuse women. Take its name: Pregnancy Counseling Center. You can see how that would be misleading. They will counsel you—but give you only one choice.

And Mellie went in there. She didn't come out for a long time, like two hours at least.

There's only one reason why she would go there.

Mellie Rivers is pregnant.

How is that even possible? Mellie wears a purity ring. She hosted a table at the Women's Day Fair promoting abstinence. She told me *to my face* that she made a commitment to herself to wait until marriage. And her parents are so conservative. They must not know. They would probably disown her. I wonder if she's told anyone.

I can't even imagine what she must be going through. I'm hugging myself as I write this, the notebook balanced on my knees. She must be so scared and feel so alone.

I want to help her. I can help her. I might be the only one who can help her.

But if I help her…

I can't.

The cost is too high.

—Lise

February 28
Dear Ms. Tilson,

My baby has a heartbeat.

I heard it today.

I didn't want to hear it.

But they made me.

I didn't want an ultrasound.

But they made me.

They made me take off my underwear and stuck a cold, lubricated wand inside me. I begged them not to. I didn't want to be touched there. The last time I was touched there was when he shoved his penis inside me. I want to forget that part of my body exists. But they made me, they made me, they made me. They said I had to hear the heartbeat to understand the decision I was making.

They said if I have an abortion, I'll get breast cancer. *Is that true?* They said I won't be able to have children. *Is that true?* It can't be. My mother had all of us. But I can't be sure of anything anymore.

They tried to give me baby clothes.

They said I should tell my parents.

They didn't believe me when I told them I was raped.

They said if I didn't go to the police when it happened, I must not be telling the truth. *Are you sure it wasn't consensual?* they asked. *Are you sure you didn't change your mind afterward? There are two sides to every story*, they said.

They said if I have an abortion, there's a chance I could die on the table. They said I could bleed to death.

They showed me pictures of aborted babies. *Don't do this*, they said.

They told me if I had the baby, I would be redeemed, forgiven for having sex outside of marriage.

They said if I had an abortion, I would get post-abortion syndrome, which would make me regret it for the rest of my life. They said I'd be at higher risk for suicide.

They said if God sent me any children in the future, I would fail to bond with them because I would feel so guilty about killing this one.

I tried to leave so many times.

They wouldn't let me leave.

They kept bringing in different counselors, all women, all wearing scrubs covered in hearts or teddy bears or storks carrying baby bundles.

They kept calling me *honey* and *dear* and *sweetie*. They kept patting my hand. One of them touched my belly. I wanted to smack her.

I can't have this baby, I told them. I don't want to have this baby.

They asked why. They didn't accept any reason I gave. I couldn't give a good enough reason. I don't want to be a mother at sixteen wasn't good enough for them. *You could give it up for adoption*, they said. *Make a childless family happy.* I said I didn't want to carry the baby of my rapist. That wasn't good enough for them. *Don't punish the baby for the sins of the father*, they said.

Somehow I got out. I still don't know how. The last two hours are a blur of Anne Geddes prints and baby clothes and shoulds and don'ts and the sound of a heartbeat beating, beating, beating, beating, beating, beating.

My baby has a heartbeat.

Signed,
Mellie Rivers

February 28
Dear Ms. Tilson—

Please don't think I'm a horrible person. You don't know what I'd be risking to help her. I can't even tell you.

I can't tell anyone.

And I definitely can't tell the daughter of our very conservative mayor whose entire political campaign could destroy—

Too much.

Just…please don't hate me for not helping her.

I have people to protect too.

—Lise

OH GOD.

OH GOD. OH GOD.

It woke me up like an earthquake.

All the pieces fell into place:

The RAINN pamphlet.

Throwing herself off the balance beam.

Crying in the bathroom for an entire class period.

Mellie Rivers isn't just pregnant.

She was raped.

She threw herself off the balance beam to try to cause a miscarriage.

If this is true, I really can help her.

But—she's the mayor's daughter. The damage she could cause…

My mind is swirling so fast that I've been sitting here for

fifteen minutes with my pen poised above the page, watching the stars, thinking. I don't know what to do.

Okay, that's not true. I know what the right thing to do is. I just don't know if I can do it.

I heard my mother get up and go to the bathroom. I almost went out into the hall to ask her what she thinks I should do. But I already know what she'd say.

I won't sleep tonight. Not a chance. When dawn comes, I know what I have to do.

—Lise

March 1
Early morning
Dear Ms. Tilson,

It's almost dawn. A thin line of blue stretches across the mountains outside my window. I've been awake all night. I wish it were possible to have a miscarriage from lack of sleep. Then I wouldn't be in this mess.

I listened to Bethany's loud breathing for hours. She's so lucky she can fall asleep anytime, anywhere. She once fell asleep on top of a pile of skis in front of the lodge while we were waiting for Dad to bring around the car. That's a skill.

Me? I have to be in a temperature-controlled room with enough white noise to be unobtrusive and just the right pillow. My brain also needs to be quiet. So, that's an issue right now. I've hardly slept in two months.

Winter was in full force last night, even though it's March. The wind howled long and close. Did you hear it? I love winter in Colorado. It's like a living thing that doesn't take orders from anyone. I wish I could be like that. Free as the wind, with the power to take down houses and uproot trees.

When it finally became clear that I could either get up or let Bethany's snoring drive me insane, I went to my closet and sat in there for a while, comforted by the warm enclosed space. I kept thinking about the Pregnancy Counseling Center. On my way there, my biggest fear was running into someone I knew from church, or around town. But all the women who worked there were strangers. They didn't care that I wouldn't give my last name. They didn't care what I wanted. All they cared about was making sure I kept the baby.

I can still hear it. In my head. The heartbeat.

I pressed my hands to my ears, but it's still there. I tried to make myself small in the corner of the closet, when something dug into my spine. I felt around in the dark. My sketchbook and pencils. I'd nearly forgotten I'd put them there, in the back of my closet, hidden away. I clutched my sketchbook and pencils and crept out of the closet.

Downstairs, the house was silent. The dining room is far enough away from the stairs that I can turn on the light without anyone seeing it, so I set up in there. I opened my sketchbook to the last thing I'd drawn, and squinted at the date. Two years ago. *Two years?* Has it really been that long? And yet…it seems like a lifetime.

The drawing was of my mother, standing at the kitchen sink, gazing out the window with faraway eyes. She hadn't noticed me, so I'd sketched quickly to capture her, not wanting to lose the moment. After I finished, I showed it to her, proud of how it had turned out. She'd pressed her lips together. "Did you finish the chicken stock?" We'd had a roast chicken for dinner that night and it was my job to make a stock from the bones afterward. When I shook my head, she sighed with annoyance. "Put away your little drawing and finish your chores, please."

That's why it's been two years since I did anything with my art.

I turned to a clean page and got out my charcoal pencils. They were still sharpened, waiting for me like an old friend. My hand hovered over the page for a long moment. What did I want to draw? What did I want to say?

Without conscious thought, my hand began to move. All that art was still in me. Those skills hadn't been lost. They had lain dormant, waiting for me to awaken them again. Drawing was an old friend. More of a friend to me than Delia, or Hannah, or even Mom.

There comes a moment when you're sketching when you just know you're done. It's like running a marathon. You know the moment you cross the finish line. When I reached that feeling, I sat back and looked at my page. The breath left my body.

I had drawn myself.

I've never done that before. I've always drawn the world around me. I've never put myself on the page. This drawing wasn't just me, though. It was me in the future. My future if I do nothing. My arms are wrapped around my swollen belly, holding myself. In another artist's hands, this might've been a sweet portrait of motherly love. In mine…the look on my face is full of anger. In the drawing, my fingers claw at the curve of my stomach, as if I want to tear the thing inside me out.

And I do.

Just as I'd captured my mother's unguarded moment, I'd captured one of my own.

"Mellie?"

I jumped out of my chair so fast it almost fell over. My father stood in the doorway in a T-shirt and his pajama bottoms. He narrowed his eyes at me. "What are you doing up?"

"I couldn't sleep."

He peered at my art supplies, and I shifted my sketchpad so he wouldn't be able to see the drawing. "Sketching again?" he asked.

"I thought it might tire me out, help me sleep."

"I had the same thought about writing my speech for the Elks Lodge." He dropped into the chair next to me. "I was hoping my own words would put me to sleep."

He smiled. I forced my lips to curve, knowing he expected me to laugh at his joke. "What's the speech about?" I asked.

"The strength of community and giving back."

"Do you ever get tired of saying the same thing over and over? Do you think anyone is listening?" The question fell out of my mouth before I could stop it.

I clamped my lips shut. We don't question Dad in our family. It was as good as the Eleventh Commandment, passed down from Mom to the rest of us. My insides clenched, waiting for the verbal blow I knew was coming.

Dad considered me in silence. That long stretch of quiet felt more dangerous than the words I'd just said.

"Of course people are listening, Mellie," he said finally. "People are listening because I make them listen. Do you know how I do that?"

I shook my head.

"Because the strength of my conviction is impossible to ignore."

Ah. It wasn't a lashing I was about to receive, but a lecture. I squirmed in my chair. "I know, Dad. You're good at your job." I made to get up, but he reached out and caught my arm.

"Show me your drawing."

I froze, my fingers hovering above the sketchpad and the secrets it held. "What?"

"Your sketch. Show me."

Once upon a time I would've shown him eagerly, in hopes of earning his praise. I pressed my hand on the pad, a gatekeeper to the secrets within. "No."

Dad's eyes widened. "Excuse me?"

"I—I don't want to show you." My mouth was dry as a desert. "It's not done."

"Show me what you've done so far."

"No," I said again. I don't think I've said the word "no" to my father twice in the same day in my life.

"Show me, Mellie."

We had entered a battle of wills, and one of us was going to walk away a loser. Dad always won, but then again, no one ever put up much of a fight. But this felt like a fight for my life, and all I knew was I couldn't let him see the drawing.

"It's not finished," I said again.

"Show me how you plan to finish it."

He was always looking to the future, never the present. "I can't. Art doesn't work that way."

He raised an eyebrow at me, like who am I for knowing how art works? "I'm not allowed to see a work in progress?" he asked.

"Would you deliver the first draft of your speech to the Elks Lodge? Or the final?"

The rest of the house may have been asleep, but my fear made everything feel awake. The vein at the base of his jaw pulsed like a light warning a ship away from a rocky shore.

"Go to bed, Mellie," he said through gritted teeth. "I hope your attitude hasn't kept me from writing this speech tonight."

That was all the lashing he was going to give me? A year

ago, a month ago, it might have cut deep, but I barely felt its sting. I took my exit and fled up the stairs. It wasn't until I got to the top that I realized I had somehow talked my way out of showing him my drawing. I tore it out of the sketchbook to hide somewhere else, just in case.

I had won, but I'd still been bruised.

Signed,
Mellie Rivers

Dear Mellie—

Do you remember the Girl Scout Law? There's a line that tells us to treat every Girl Scout like a sister. You may have left Girl Scouts all those years ago, but I never stopped being your sister.

I think I know what's going on with you, and I can help.

Don't go back to the PCC. I can take you someplace where you can get real care.

Please trust me.

I haven't said anything to anyone and I won't, I promise.

I'm here for you whenever you are ready.

Love,

—Lise

March 1
Night
Dear Ms. Tilson,

Lise Grant left a note in my locker this morning. "Don't go back to the PCC."

She saw me.

Does she know my secret?

She must. Why else would I go into a pregnancy clinic? Oh God, oh God, oh God. How did she see me? Was she following me? Is she *spying* on me?

And why is she calling the PCC by its initials like she's on a first-name basis with it or something?

And then she had the nerve to say "I never stopped being your sister." We were in the same Girl Scout troop a million years ago. "Please trust me"? Who does she think she is? Why would I trust her? I've barely talked to Lise Grant in ten years. Why on earth would I turn to her, of all people?

Although, it's not like I can turn to anyone else.

I don't know why she thinks she can help me. No one can help me.

Signed,
Mellie Rivers

Dear Lise,

Thank you, but you can't help me.

Please forget whatever you think you saw.

Mellie

Dear Mellie—

If you don't want help, that's fine...but something tells me you *need* help and don't know how to get it. *That*, I can help with.

At least let me tell you how I can help. I'd rather tell you in person than in a note. Write back a time and place we can meet.

—Lise

Lise,

Meet me today after school in the girls' bathroom by the gym.

Mellie

March 2

Dear Ms. Tilson,

The girls' bathroom near the gym smelled like smoke, but it was empty except for Lise when I pushed open the door. I didn't know why I was there. Why I agreed to meet her. Was I really going to tell her the truth? To say out loud all I've been writing down in this journal? I didn't plan to. I think, mainly, I went out of curiosity, to see if she really could help me.

Lise was already there, leaning against one of the sinks. After she locked the door—which I didn't know you could do—she spread out a long scarf for us to sit on. "I came prepared this time," she said. "My ass was freezing that day I sat in here with you."

She leaned back against the wall by the last stall and looked at me. The memory of being in that stall with her on the other side was sharp, how her hand was so close to mine, separated by a breath and an invisible wall of all our differences. I looked back at her for what felt like a long time.

Then, I sat. I pulled my knees up against my chest. "I don't know where to start," I whispered.

"You don't have to start anywhere," Lise said. "We can just sit here if you want."

Something inside me cracked a little. She was being the true kind of friend, the kind that cares about you without making it all about them. I remembered how she'd stood up for Delia without expecting anything in return.

But I didn't have time to sit and cry in the bathroom anymore. Every day I crossed off on the *Virgin of the Rocks* calendar was one day closer to not having a choice. "No. I need to tell someone."

Lise leaned toward me, her shoulder touching mine. "Tell me why you went to the Pregnancy Counseling Center."

I turned my head to face her, my cheek resting on my knees. "I think you know why."

She brought her knees up so that we were like mirror statues. "How far along are you?"

"They said twelve weeks."

"That's still early," Lise said. "You still have a lot of options."

Options, options, options... I'm so sick of hearing that word. I don't feel like I have options. I see three paths in front of me and all of them look bad.

"Mellie." She said it soft and gentle, like harp music in church, and reached out to touch my fingers. "Were you raped?"

I tightened myself into a smaller ball. I could not get small enough. My throat constricted. All I could do was nod.

"Oh, Mellie," she said. "I'm so sorry that happened to you."

Tears spilled from my eyes. Finally, the words I wanted to hear. *I'm sorry that happened to you.* I didn't want anyone's pity, but I wanted someone to acknowledge that what had happened on that basement floor was terrible and wrong. Not even the women at the PCC had said they were sorry. They called me a liar.

Lise's fingers tightened on mine. "Who was it?"

My gut clenched. "I can't say."

"Mellie, he doesn't deserve your protection. He's the one who did something wrong, not you."

"No." The word cut the air between us. "I'm not protecting him. That's all I'm gonna say."

She closed her eyes for a long moment. "Okay. Fine. That's your choice."

It's just the way things are.

Lise opened her eyes. "What did they tell you at the PCC?"

I took a long ragged breath, and then I told her. I told her everything they said about cancer and infertility, God and Jesus, post-abortion syndrome and regret, and options. Except they were only offering one option: have the baby. It felt like I'd been carrying glass in my mouth, and when I was finally done talking, I'd spit all the glass out.

"First of all, most of what they told you are lies. Abortion doesn't cause cancer or infertility. And there's no such thing as post-abortion syndrome." She made a gagging sound. "That makes me want to punch those bitches."

I wished I'd had the courage to do that. My hands trembled. "They gave me an ultrasound. Made me listen to the baby's heartbeat."

"Oh, Mellie."

Breath choked in my throat. "How can I kill something that has a heartbeat?"

She turned so she was on her knees and put her arms around me. I buried my face into her shoulder and cried. I cried for that tiny little heartbeat, cried for my own heartbeat, cried because it was the first time since this nightmare began that someone had comforted me.

"It's gonna be okay," she murmured. "Everything's going to be okay."

"How?" I pulled back a little, tears still streaming down my face. "How is it going to be okay? I want to get rid of it. But how am I going to live with myself after that?"

Lise pressed her mouth into a straight line. "I wish I had the answer to that, Mellie. I really do."

My heart fell. For a moment, I'd really thought she could help me.

"But," she went on, and my heart lifted again, "if you do want an abortion, or if you want to hear what your real options are without the judging and shaming you got at the PCC, I can help you with that."

"How?"

"You trusted me," she said. "I have to trust you too."

"Trust me with what?"

She looked down at our clasped hands. "I've never told anyone this, Mellie. Not even Cara, or Rowan. I've wanted to, but…it's not safe."

I tried to pull my hand away, but she didn't let go. "Whatever it is, Lise, you don't have to tell me." That was a lie. I desperately wanted to know what she had to say.

"No. I want to tell you." She swallowed hard. "It had to be the right person, someone who needs to know rather than just wanted to know, if that makes sense."

I nodded.

"I've never said this out loud," she said. "My mom can help you. She's the head doctor at Whole Women's Health Clinic."

I felt her confession deep in my gut, Ms. Tilson. It was as deep as what I'd confessed to Lise. I understood what it cost her to tell me—*me*, the daughter of the man who wants that clinic and all the others like it closed. Tears welled up behind my eyes.

For once I was crying for someone else, not for me. "I'm sorry, Lise. I'm so sorry for everything my dad's ever said about that clinic and all the doctors."

Lise squeezed my hand and leaned toward me. "Mellie, you can't tell him. He doesn't know it's her. You have no idea what we go through to protect her identity," she went on. I could hear the angry tears in her voice. "Fake names on the payroll, a guarded underground entrance so she can't be followed in and out… All so people like your dad won't harass her…or worse." She let go of my hand and gripped my upper arms. "You have to promise me you won't tell your dad or anyone, Mellie. You know what happened at that clinic in Minneapolis last year, don't you?"

"Yes," I whispered. Five people shot, three killed. I remember watching the report on the news with my dad and saying, "Doesn't killing people defeat the purpose of being pro-life?" My dad had given me a withering look, like I didn't understand the complexity of the situation.

"Promise me," Lise said.

I looked her in the eyes. A year ago, I might not have made that promise. But now…my mind flashed to that stage in Woodview, to my dad saying you can't get pregnant from rape. "I promise," I said. (Except now I've told you. I needed to write it down. Maybe I'll tear these pages out before I hand in this journal.)

Lise pulled me into a tight hug. "Thank you," she whispered into my ear. "And I promise, Mellie, I'll get you to my mom's clinic. We'll help you."

And finally, I believed her.

Signed,
Mellie Rivers

March 2
Dear Ms. Tilson—

It's a strange feeling, telling someone a secret you've been holding so close for so long. At first you think it's going to drown you, but then you realize the water is actually lifting you up. After what she told me, I would be a hypocrite if I didn't offer up my own deeply held truth. Especially when I know it can help her. That gut feeling I had was leading me to this moment.

I had to tell Mellie, but I want to tell you my secret too. This journal will never be honest without it. After all you've said about feminism in class, I believe you're on our side. Plus, you have a Michelle Obama poster on your wall.

My mother is the head doctor at Whole Women's Health. Less than ten people in town know this: the staff at the clinic, me, and the driver who picks her up from a different secure location every day and delivers her to the underground entrance so she doesn't get harassed—or worse—by the protesters outside. And now Mellie knows. And you.

Not even Rowan knows.

A year or so ago he asked me why my parents got divorced. And I told him they were fighting all the time, they fell out of love, blah blah blah. I said all the typical stuff people cough up when their parents get divorced. But the main reason they got divorced was because of my mom's work.

It's not because my dad is anti-choice. He's not. He said he couldn't compete with all my mom's patients. He was tired of coming in second.

I overheard them fighting one night, after they thought I'd gone to bed. It was shortly before they told me they were getting a divorce. It must have been their last big fight. A lot of mean, ugly things were said. I heard it all.

My dad accused my mom of loving her work more than him, of making her patients a higher priority than her own family. (For the record, I've *never* felt that way about my mom. I know I come first.)

Then my mom accused my dad of wanting some version of a 1950s wife who greets him at the door wearing an apron and puts his slippers on his feet while he reads the paper. My dad got superloud and defensive after my mom said this. Probably because, deep down, there's a grain of truth there.

Things got uglier and meaner from there until it went silent.

I remember standing at the top of the stairs, listening hard. I tiptoed down a few steps, hoping I'd find them kissing, like so many other fights.

They were on opposite sides of the room. My dad sat on the couch with his head in his hands. My mom leaned against the wall, like she was trying to hold herself up. One of them said, "I think this is it," in such a hoarse, harsh whisper that I couldn't tell who was speaking. "I think it is," the other one answered. I turned and fled back up the stairs. A week later, they gave me the news.

Now my dad lives in New Mexico. He has a girlfriend who he's probably going to marry. Meanwhile, my mom still lives alone (well, with me) in this smallish town, working eleven hours a day. We both pitch in taking care of the house, and I never feel like I come in second. It's ironic that my dad accused my mom of not making me a priority when he's the parent who makes me feel like that.

My mom and I are always honest with each other. I have to tell my mom that I told Mellie about her and the clinic. She needs to know exactly who knows her identity, because if anything ever happens, the police will need to know to figure out who the snitch was. I need to tell her about Mellie too. I know she'll want to help her like I do.

But even if I get her into the clinic, even if Mom helps her, that's only the start. She still has a long road to walk, and I can't walk it for her. The best I can do is walk beside her so that she always knows I'm there.

—Lise

March 4
Dear Ms. Tilson,

I used to love church. It was fun to see family friends, especially Delia. With her dad up there preaching, it made me feel special that we were close with the pastor and his family, part of the inner circle. It was as if that brought us even closer to God. I would always sing full-out, filled with the Holy Spirit. The organ was so loud it had to be impossible for God not to hear. The candles, the light pouring in through the stained-glass windows… I remember thinking how romantic it was. I could totally understand why Catholic women wanted to become nuns. Who wouldn't want to spend their lives in this beautiful place?

Now it's all so ugly to me.

HE is there.

I try so hard to not look at him, to act as if he didn't destroy me.

I don't want to give him any more power than he already has.

He ignores me, of course. I'm nothing to him, nothing but

a body he used for his own pleasure one time. Maybe he doesn't even remember. Maybe he's done this to other girls and we all blend together for him.

Mom noticed me not singing and raised her eyebrows at me. I pretended to be interested in my hymnal and moved my mouth just enough to get her off my case. A panicky flutter started in the base of my gut and tightened through my chest so that it was hard to breathe. I looked up at all the bent heads around me, and suddenly I saw sheep, all bleating the same tune. I needed to get out.

Bethany raised her head and stared at me. "What's wrong?" she mouthed.

I fanned my face. I couldn't breathe. Bethany just rolled her eyes. "Stop being so dramatic," she whispered and started singing again.

I forced air into my lungs. The hymn ended and we sat down. Pastor Charlie started his sermon. It dragged on for hours. Days might have passed inside that church. It's so hard to listen to him now. I can't see him as anything other than a hypocrite. I closed my eyes, arranging my face into an expression that hopefully looked like I was absorbing the sermon. To keep calm, I started listing all the states in alphabetical order in my head.

Somewhere around Michigan, I heard it.

"Abortion."

My eyes flew open.

"We are so fortunate to have a mayor who is fighting to preserve the sanctity of life." Pastor Charlie nodded toward my dad. "We here at Word of Life Church will be supporting him in the upcoming election."

The back of my neck grew itchy. Among all the other things I notice now, I notice how often Pastor Charlie talks about my dad, how blurry the lines are between church and state. Dad talks about how there shouldn't be a line between the two, that Christian principles should always be taken into consideration when making laws. Then he'll talk about upholding the Constitution in the next breath.

We had a debate about this topic last month in American History. And I think those two things are mutually exclusive.

"Banning abortion in Colorado will be Hiram Rivers's top priority in office, just as it is a top priority for all of us here at Word of Life."

I couldn't list the states in my head anymore; Pastor Charlie's voice had gotten in and there was no getting it out. My legs trembled. I held my knee to make it stop. We were pressed so close in the pew that Mom or Bethany would surely notice.

"It is a source of deep shame that one of the state's last remaining abortion clinics is right here in our beloved town." Pastor Charlie's gaze swept across the congregation. Was it my imagination or did he stop on me for an instant? "They may claim to care about women's health, but we here at Word of Life know the truth. We know what goes on behind those closed doors. It is a factory of death. The floors are covered with the blood of innocent babies, and everyone who works there is an instrument of Satan."

Unlike the campaign rally in Woodview, everyone here nodded along. The judgment surrounded me. In the row in front of us, where the Bellows family sat, Mrs. Bellows raised her hand to the air and gave a loud "Amen."

"Many of you are doing God's work by talking to women as they approach this clinic, educating them about what really happens inside." Pastor Charlie offered a smile, nodding at a few people in the pews. "And while this work is important, it is time that we take further steps toward preserving the sanctity of life. It is not enough to convince women not to go into these clinics." He grasped the edges of the lectern and leaned forward, his mouth so close to the microphone that his voice reverberated off the walls. "We must prevent the people who work in these clinics from doing Satan's work."

All my body's warmth drained away and left me freezing cold. He may have couched it in flowery words, but I knew what he was saying. I knew what he was inciting people to do. My mind flashed to the news footage from the clinic in Minnesota, the black body bags being rolled out the front door on stretchers…

He wants that to happen here.

He wants that to happen to Lise's mom.

When Lise told me about her mom, it seemed like an abstract danger. But today it became a concrete threat. I'm so scared for her, for her mom—more scared than I was sitting in that church with HIM so close by.

Even God can't keep evil out of His own house.

After the service, I tried to escape fast, but the crowd was thick and we were stuck in our pew. Mrs. Bellows stopped Mom to talk to her about Hannah's bridal shower, and I couldn't get around her. Pastor Charlie moved down the aisle, greeting people, clapping Dad on the back when he passed him. My dad was in full networking mode, pressing flesh with anyone in reaching distance. A lot of people offered to help out on his campaign, and he directed them to his website—where they could volunteer and donate money.

We finally made it into the aisle.

And I came face-to-face with HIM.

There were people all around me. I couldn't turn away.

He smiled at me.

I stared at him. I wanted to claw that smug, satisfied smile off his face, leave him scarred like he's forever scarred me.

He leaned into me. His hot breath was on my neck. "I had a great time at your house at Christmas," he whispered, so quiet only I could hear. His hand touched mine. To anyone around us, it probably looked like he was shaking my hand and maybe giving me a friendly peck on the cheek. "I hope we can do it again sometime."

Then he was gone so fast I started to doubt it had even happened.

But it did. I'm writing about it because it happened.

Not only does he remember, he remembers it HIS way, not mine. He thinks I liked it. He thinks it was consensual. And everyone else will too. They'll believe him, not me.

What I'm writing here in these pages—this is the truth. No matter what anyone says, I know what's true, and it's all right here in black and white.

Signed,
Mellie Rivers

March 5
Dear Ms. Tilson,

It is March. This month our Women of the Bible calendar features Judith and Holofernes. Judith does not appear in the Bible, but in the Apocrypha, a sort of Bible companion book. The painting depicts her at the exact moment of slaughtering Holofernes, the cruel general who has imprisoned her city. Her knife is at his throat and there is blood everywhere as she saws his head off.

My favorite part of this painting is that it was done by a woman. There's a little note about the artist underneath the Biblical text crediting it to Artemisia Gentileschi, daughter of the famous Renaissance artist Orazio Gentileschi. (Why they had to mention her father at all, I don't know. Didn't she paint it all by herself, without his help?) I looked her up in one of the *Art of the Western World* books in the school library this afternoon. Artemisia was famous in her own right, second only to Caravaggio in her time. But she wasn't only famous for her art.

She was famous because she'd been raped and her father took her rapist to court. At the time, most girls would've kept their shame silent or their families might have sent them to a convent to lessen the disgrace. Instead, her father fought for her…and won.

Knowing this, I stared at the painting for a long time when I got home today. I wondered, was she thinking about her rapist when she painted it? Did Holofernes bear the face of the man who violated her? Was she painting her revenge through Judith?

I think she was. I think she poured everything that happened to her into her art.

I want to paint like that someday.

Signed,
Mellie Rivers

March 6
Dear Ms. Tilson—

This afternoon, Rowan came over and we hardcore made out on the couch. Like half my clothes were off and half his clothes were off, and his hands were all over me. I wanted them all over me. At one point, he pulled away and reached into his backpack that was on the floor next to the couch. He pulled out a condom.

"Do you want to?" he asked, his voice all raspy.

I wanted to. I wanted to take off the rest of our clothes and be totally naked with him. To feel his skin against mine and have him inside me. *I wanted that.*

I was about to say yes, when suddenly Mellie's voice was in my head.

How can I kill something with a heartbeat?

Condoms are only effective about 97 percent of the time, so there was a 3 percent chance that I could get pregnant with

Rowan. Maybe it was only 3 percent, but was I ready if I had to deal with that?

I sat up and put my head in my hands.

Rowan sat up too. "It's okay," he said.

(I told you he was a good guy. The best kind of guy.)

I looked up into his face and touched his cheek. "I'm not ready. I'm sorry."

"Don't be sorry. This isn't something you have to be sorry for."

I kissed him hard, long, and deep, breathing "thank you" into his mouth. Thank you for understanding. Thank you for not being a dickwad like Jason Bellows or the asshole who raped Mellie.

Then we did some stuff I had never done before. It wasn't sex, but felt just as intimate. I super enjoyed it, but that's all I'm going to tell you.

:)

By the time my mom got home, we were fully clothed and doing our homework at the kitchen table like a pair of perfect students. Rowan stayed for dinner, and after dinner he *did the dishes*. If I didn't love him before, I definitely do now. But I am really glad we didn't have sex. Because if I can't deal with what could come afterward, then I'm definitely not ready.

After he left, my mom turned to me. "Did you two have sex this afternoon?"

I swear to God, I almost died. How did she know?! What

kind of mom superpower is that? My jaw hit the floor, and I sputtered for a few seconds. Then, because I never lie to my mom, I told her the truth. I told her about almost doing it, then choosing not to, and how Rowan respected my choice. I told her about the not-sex stuff we did, even though it made me totally red in the face to talk about and I couldn't look at her while I told her.

Mom took my hand when I was done. "Thank you for being honest with me, Lise." She squeezed my fingers. "I think you made the right choice, but when the time comes, I trust you to know what you are doing."

"Thanks, Mom."

We hugged it out. She was about to get up from the couch, but I stopped her.

I told her about Mellie.

"That poor girl," she said, running her fingers through her hair. "She probably feels so alone. Especially...given who her family is." She sighed. "I have to be honest. I don't like the idea of someone so close to Hiram Rivers knowing about me."

"I know, Mom. But I couldn't *not* help her." My throat was tight. It gets that way a lot when I think about Mellie.

"Of course you couldn't," she said, touching my knee. "I'm proud of you for helping her. And if you say she won't tell, we have to trust that she won't. We just need to be extra vigilant. I'll make sure Jasmine knows." She chewed her lip. "At any rate, whatever night she can get away, I'll see her. Just shoot me a text during the day and I'll get Daphne to pick you guys up." She got up from the couch. Halfway to the stairs, she turned back to me. "Lise."

"Yeah?"

"Does she know about the forty-eight hours?"

I closed my eyes. I didn't know. She was so scared that I had been afraid to ask her. "I don't think so, Mom."

"We'll talk about all her options when she comes in." She climbed the stairs, disappearing down the hallway at the top.

Her options. What did that even mean for Mellie? Once she heard about the forty-eight–hour law, she would freak out.

It wasn't fair. I wanted to throw something, smash it against the wall like it's the patriarchy.

Everyone worries about their precious boys, their lives ruined if they're accused of rape. Never understanding that it's the girls who have ruined lives now—internal scars that will never heal, sometimes a baby forced on them that they never asked for. But somehow, it's all our fault.

Abstinence *only*, they teach us in school. But if we don't put out, we're prudes. And if we do, we're sluts. There are too many rules to follow, and I can't keep track of them all. I'm still just a girl, but I'm starting to feel how hard it is to be a woman in this world.

It feels like there's a brick wall we have to break through

to be considered equal to men, and every time a crack becomes wide enough to fit through, it gets cemented over.

I want to be one of the women to help break through that wall, then protect it so no one can cement it shut again, and me and Mellie and Cara and all the other girls—yes, all, even Delia—can get through.

—Lise

March 6
Night
Dear Ms. Tilson,

Today at lunch Lise found me in the cafeteria annex. We got a few looks, mainly because people don't usually sit together in the annex. The annex is for losers who have lost all their friends and have to sit by themselves.

"Where's Cara?" I asked.

Lise shrugged. "I told her I'd be sitting with you. She was cool."

I wonder what that's like, having friends who are cool when you do things your own way once in a while. I pushed my fork through my mac and cheese. When I chose it on the lunch line, it looked delicious, but now the smell was turning my stomach. I took a swig of water instead.

"How are you feeling?" Lise asked.

"Nauseous. All the time." I glanced around and lowered my voice even more. "I can't believe people do this voluntarily."

"No argument from me." Lise took a big bite of her hamburger. I almost gagged. When she was done chewing, she spoke again. "I talked to my mom—"

My stomach did a little flip-flop. "You told your mom?"

Lise's face scrunched up. "Oh, Mellie, I'm sorry. I did. I had to in order to let her know—"

"No, no, it's okay. I mean, it's not like she wasn't going to find out."

"Yeah, that's true. She said she can see you whenever you're ready."

I nodded, again looking around to make sure no one was listening. They weren't. Most of the kids had on headphones anyway.

"Probably after hours would be better," Lise went on. "Do you think you could get away in the evening, like seven?"

"I…I don't know," I said. "I'd have to come up with a really good reason. It might be hard."

"I'm sure we'll figure something out."

"Okay," I whispered. My heart was beating fast, like millions of tiny hummingbird wings. As long as I just talk about it, it's not real. Making a plan feels too real, too fast. But I can't wait much longer.

I already have a bump.

Hannah had a wedding dress fitting this afternoon, and I had to go get my maid of honor dress fitted at the same visit.

Hannah chose her dress several months ago, and they had to order it. Me and Mom and Bethany were all with her when she chose it, and we all cried when they put the veil on her, just like on all those wedding dress shows on television. It seems so far out of the realm of memory now.

Bethany and I are co-maids of honor, and our dresses are slightly different from the ones that Delia and Ruth will wear as bridesmaids, and Joanie, who's the flower girl. The dresses are the most beautiful shade of pink—dusty rose, it's called—with a princess skirt and three-quarter–length sleeves that are trimmed with floral embroidery. I remember feeling so pretty and important the day we picked these dresses out.

Today as Hannah was being fitted in one dressing room, I was pulling on my maid of honor dress in another. Like Hannah's wedding dress, our dresses were specially ordered, custom-sized to fit our measurements.

"How's it going?" Hannah called from her room.

"Great!" Bethany called back from her room on the other side of me.

In the middle of them, I was silent. I could barely get the dress on. I was able to get it over my hips but it would only zip a few inches. Sweat trickled down my neck and armpits as I tried to force the zipper. It wouldn't budge.

"Okay," said Vera, the seamstress, in her Russian accent, after finishing with Hannah. I heard the curtain slide open. "Let's see how the beautiful maids are doing." Before I could stop her, Vera stepped into my room. Thankfully my mother was in Hannah's room and not sitting on the couch on the other side of the curtain where she could see me.

I spun to face Vera, my arms twisted behind me, clutching both sides of the zipper. Out of the corner of my eye, I could see my reflection in the mirror, my hair mussed and stuck to my sweaty face, my eyes wide and scared. She took one long survey of my body, and I saw my own panic reflected in her eyes.

She knew. She works with women's bodies all day long; I shouldn't be surprised she knew.

"Please," I mouthed to her, shaking my head, more hair falling across my face.

"Okay, good," she said loudly. Swiftly, she clipped the curtain to the walls so that no one could come in. Then her deft hands pushed mine out of the way and worked up and down the dress, ripping open seams, pinning and folding fabric so that within a matter of minutes, the dress was fitted to me. She raised the waistline just enough to hide the slight bulge of my belly, widened the neckline to allow for my swelling breasts. When she was done, she stepped back and examined her work. "Voilà," she said softly.

My chin trembled. Tears spilled onto my cheeks. "Thank you," I whispered, so quiet that only she could hear me. She put her arm around me and drew my head to her shoulder, letting me sob silently for a moment.

"It will be okay," she breathed into my ear. Then she slipped out of my room and into Bethany's, leaving me alone to compose myself before my mother came in to pick me apart.

I can't rely on the Veras of the world to hide me much longer. I can't just think about doing something. I have to do it before everyone knows.

Signed,
Mellie Rivers

March 7
Dear Ms. Tilson,

In between all the nausea, I crave things. Deep intense cravings that wake me up in the middle of the night. Two nights ago, I tiptoed downstairs and ate all the Fudgsicles. Joanie is the only one who eats them, and the next night, when my mom went to get one for her after dinner, there was a huge crisis in the kitchen when she discovered they were all gone. Joanie threw a tantrum, Mom accused all of us of eating them, and I lied so well I should've won an Oscar.

I didn't throw up the Fudgsicles. Mom's roasted chicken with potatoes and carrots? That only stayed down about fifteen minutes after dinner.

Today during your class, Ms. Tilson, the gnawing started in my gut, eating away at me until by the end of school it was a full-on craving, so strong I couldn't think about anything else. I literally couldn't remember my locker combination because this craving had taken over my brain. You know Marie's? They make the best carrot cake in the world. Dense and moist and with cream cheese frosting that's inches thick, exactly the way carrot cake should be. I could not stop thinking about it. I could taste it in my mouth. I *needed* it.

Technically, I'm allowed to go out after school; it's just understood that if I do, it has to be to the library or church or Delia's house. So when I met Bethany on the steps outside school, I told her the truth. "I'm craving that carrot cake from Marie's. I'll be home in an hour or so."

"Oh, yum," Bethany said. "I'd come with you if it wasn't for my piano lesson. Bring me a piece?"

"Sure."

She went in one direction and I went in the other.

I barely made it half a block when Lise caught up to me. "Are you stalking me?" I asked her.

Her face turned red. "Okay, I kinda followed you last week, but I wasn't today."

I stopped and stared at her. "I was kidding! You've actually been stalking me?"

"I knew something was up… I couldn't let it go."

Maybe I should've been annoyed with her, but Lise is the only one I can talk to right now. So I rolled my eyes and started walking again. Lise fell into step with me. "I'm going to Marie's," I told her before she could ask. "I need a piece of carrot cake."

"Yuck. There is something wrong with putting vegetables in cake."

"You don't notice the vegetables when there's that much frosting involved."

Lise laughed.

When we got to Marie's, it was practically empty. It doesn't get much of an after-school crowd. Most of the kids go to Starbucks, which, thankfully, hasn't driven Marie's out of business. I got two slices of carrot cake (one for me and one to go for Bethany) and Lise got a red velvet cupcake. When I took my first bite of cake, it was as if everything I'd ever eaten had been sawdust. *Nothing* ever tasted that good. I think I may have actually moaned. Lise stared at me. I told her about the Fudgsicle incident.

We sat there for more than an hour, talking and laughing like we were just two totally normal friends getting their afternoon sugar fix. It felt so good, Ms. Tilson. It felt safe. I could be myself and not have to worry about covering up this terrible secret I'm keeping. In the span of a few days, Lise has become a better friend than Delia ever was. She cares about me for *me*, not because of who my family is or what I can do for her.

I elbowed Lise. "Hey. Thanks for stalking me."

She elbowed me back. "Hey. You're welcome."

She didn't ask me what I was going to do about my situation, or how I was feeling, or if had I changed my mind about reporting what happened. This afternoon she was just my friend. It wasn't until we left that I understood how much I needed that.

Signed,
Mellie Rivers

March 7

Dear Ms. Tilson—

This afternoon Mellie and I got our sugar on at Marie's (which thankfully Starbucks hasn't put out of business) and talked like two old friends. You know what? She's awesome. I guess I've always had this idea that she's a little high and mighty, or that she thinks she's better than everyone else. Why did I think that? Why did I assume that, instead of getting to know her? I've always prided myself on being open-minded and tolerant…but maybe I'm only tolerant of people who think like me.

The funny thing is, Mellie is a lot more like me than I thought.

What she's going through is changing her. I can see it. There's a privilege in being a witness to it. Because when all is said and done, there will probably be very few people who will know her before and after like I will. I just hope her family sticks by her. I can't imagine going through life without my mom. Nobody should have to know what that's like.

My dad called me tonight. I totally forgot I was supposed to visit him this weekend. I told him I had to wait until next month. I just feel like…I don't know…I need to be here. In case Mellie needs me.

Dad was pretty upset. He went into a whole long monologue about making a commitment and sticking to it. What he doesn't understand is that I *am* making a commitment and sticking to it—it's just to Mellie and not to him. Finally I put the phone on speaker so Mom could hear, and set it on the kitchen table. After a minute, she picked it up and interrupted him. I don't know what she said because she carried the phone into the other room, but I got the strong sense that I shouldn't follow. When she came back, she just handed me the phone. Dad cleared his throat, said he'd miss me, and that he'd call the airline to change the flights for next month.

This is why I don't watch superhero movies and TV shows. I already have a superhero in my own home.

—Lise

March 9
Dear Ms. Tilson,

The bathroom by the gym has become one of the few safe spaces I have left. I don't know what it is about that bathroom. It's like a sanctuary of pink tile and graffiti. There are curse words written in all the stalls, about girls long since graduated, that the janitor hasn't been able to scrub out. An old nail polish stain distorts one of the mirrors. The tile is chipped and the heater clangs. All these things drive other girls from here, giving me a place to be myself.

Maybe it's not the bathroom. Maybe it's because Lise is here too.

When we were settled on her scarf, she pulled out a package of almonds and offered them to me. I cupped my hands and she poured a little pile. I ate them one by one, chewing slowly to make sure they were not going to come up again.

"I haven't figured out a good excuse to get out of the house," I told her. "I will soon."

"You could tell your parents you're having dinner at my house."

I shook my head. "They don't let me have dinner with people they don't know. They'll ask me a million questions about you and your mom, the first being 'Where do they go to church?'"

"Then tell them you're having dinner at someone else's house. Someone they've already approved."

"I'd have to get that person to cover for me. No, it needs to be something where no one else has to lie for me."

Lise tapped her finger against her lips. "I wish Mom could get you in during regular hours after school, but she's booked solid for the next month. Hey, can you suddenly start taking a pottery class?"

I raised my eyebrows at her.

"Yeah, that's not a great excuse. Okay, we'll figure something out. But we gotta do it soon."

I ran my fingers through my hair, pulling tight on the strands. "I can't wait much longer, can I?"

"You can get an abortion up to thirty-six weeks in Colorado," Lise said. I stared at her. "But my mom doesn't do them past twenty weeks unless something is wrong with the baby or the mother's life is in immediate danger."

"Thirty-six weeks? God, that's...that's...a baby," I choked out. I remembered what my mother looked like when she was thirty-six weeks pregnant with my sisters, big and heavy. She'd let us touch her belly to feel how active the baby was inside.

"I escorted a woman who was thirty-two weeks," Lise said softly. "She said her baby's brain developed outside of its skull. There was nothing the doctors could do. It was going to die when it was born. But that doesn't make it any less sad." Her voice cracked a little.

I tried to imagine hearing that news: that the baby you loved and were waiting for was going to die. Why would God do that to someone? I guess the same way He'd allowed me to be raped and get pregnant. I'd never realized before how cruel life could be.

"I can't wait until twenty weeks," I told her. "Everyone will know soon. My parents can't know."

"Mellie," Lise said, and I could tell she was choosing her words carefully, "what would happen if they knew?"

A million responses ran through my head. My parents would say that somehow it was my fault. Even if they believed me about the rape, they would say I was bringing shame to the family. They would say I was damaging my dad's campaign by creating a scandal. And they would make me keep the baby. That I knew for certain. They would probably lock me up somewhere for the duration of my pregnancy, so no one would find out. Maybe my mom would claim the baby was hers, like the plot on a soap opera.

They would hold this over me for the rest of my life, the way I tried to bring them all down and how they saved me.

But I didn't say any of this to Lise.

"They can't know," I said again, and left it at that.

She looked like she wanted to say something more, but didn't. Just as well. There is nothing she could say to convince me to tell my parents.

Writing this now, with a flashlight in my closet (another safe space) while Bethany sleeps, I feel the deep truth of it. My parents can never know. They can never know about the rape, or the pregnancy, or what I am finally ready to do.

Signed,
Mellie Rivers

March 12
Dear Ms. Tilson—

This afternoon I met Mellie in the library, in one of the tucked-away corners people rarely go to unless they're desperate to make out. It's not the best make-out spot in the school (that's the costume storage room behind the stage in the auditorium), but sometimes the storage room is occupied and you have to take what you can get.

After Mellie and I had settled into those low, squishy chairs, she turned to me. "I'm ready," she said. "I'm ready to see your mom."

I put my hand on her arm. "You're sure?"

She nodded. Her eyes looked overbright, but I had to take her word for it. "Can we go tonight?" she asked.

"Yeah—crap, no." I tugged at my hair. "My mom has her staff meeting on Monday nights after the clinic closes."

Mellie sucked in a breath and her eyes grew more shiny. I

squeezed her forearm. "Can you make it tomorrow? Do you have your excuse ready?"

"I…I didn't say anything to my parents yet."

I looked at her. She couldn't quite meet my eyes. "You don't have an excuse yet."

She pressed her fingers to her temple. "My brain. My brain won't work no matter how hard I try to come up with an excuse for them."

"We'll figure something out." I mean, what the hell else could I say? What do you say to a girl who is always expected home by six for dinner?

We were quiet for a long time while we both thought really hard. Seriously, I think I could actually hear our brains tick-tick-ticking away. After a while, Mellie pulled out a sketchbook from her bag and started to draw. "It helps me think," she said.

I watched her hand move in long, sweeping lines across the page. She had the pad turned away from me so I couldn't see what she was drawing, but I couldn't stop watching her. Remember when I said there always used to be an aura around her? While she was sketching, that light came back. Her whole face glowed as her hand moved across the page. She's like a different person when she draws.

Then it hit me. She's not a different person when she sketches, she's her true self. This is who she truly is.

I pulled my knees up under my chin and watched her. I don't

think she was aware I was staring at her. She was in her own world, far away, in the other dimension of whatever she was creating on her page. I wish I had a passion like that. I wish I had something that was purely mine, something so deep and true that I couldn't *not* do it. I don't feel that way about anything, really.

At that moment I envied Mellie Rivers.

There was a rustling in the stacks beside us and the spell broke. Mellie's hand paused and we both looked up as Rowan crashed into our cozy corner.

"There you are!" he said. "Oh, hey—Mellie, right?" He glanced at me, a swift, almost-invisible look. I knew he was remembering our conversation at dinner, but I gave him a look back, hoping he wouldn't say anything about that. Amazingly, he seemed to get it. He peered over Mellie's shoulder at her drawing, and before I could tell him not to invade her private artist's space, he said, "Whoa. That's amazing!"

Mellie tilted the sketchpad toward her chest to hide it. "No, it's nothing."

"Are you kidding? You are really talented. May I?" He held out his hand and smiled, making that little dimple in his right cheek appear. He was probably in the library looking for me because he wanted to make out in this very corner (which, okay, we've done before), and all of a sudden I wanted to make out with him, too.

Slowly, Mellie lifted the sketchpad and handed it to Rowan. He dropped down to sit on the floor next to me, all lanky limbs and moppish hair. He flipped through a couple of pages, looking at all of them intently. "The way you play with light and shadow is so interesting. I've never seen anything like it. It's like you bring everything that's usually in shadow into the light, and put everything into shadow that's normally in light."

"I…I've never thought about it like that. I just draw the world like I see it."

Rowan lifted his gaze from the book and grinned at Mellie. "You should really show this to my mom."

"Your mom?"

"Oh yeah," I said. "She runs the Empty Space. You know, the art gallery in town."

"I've never been there," Mellie said.

"Yeah, it's mostly for tourists," Rowan said. "But she loves nurturing young artists. She does a residency program every summer. You should totally apply." He tilted the pad so I could see Mellie's drawing too.

My breath caught in my lungs.

My heart squeezed.

She had drawn herself inside a cage. She was trapped, and the look on her face was one of defeat, surrender. I'd never seen a sadder picture. In the picture, Mellie's fingers curled around the bars, as though she wanted to break out, but her eyes were downcast, as if she knew she could not escape. "Oh, Mellie," I breathed. I felt her and Rowan's gaze on me. I forced myself to swallow past the lump in my throat. "It's beautiful."

"See?" Rowan said. "You have to meet my mom."

"I…I don't know."

"Oh, come on! Here." Rowan dug into his backpack and pulled out a glossy flyer. "They're having an opening tomorrow night for a new artist from Boulder. You can come and meet my mom. There'll even be free food."

He thrust the flyer into Mellie's hands. She and I bent over it, our heads touching as we read.

America: Lost & Found

Mixed-media photographs by Lee Skyler

Tuesday, March 13 from 7 to 10 p.m.

Mellie and I raised our heads and looked at each other.

7 to 10 p.m.

A public event at a public place where no one will notice if we show up late, or how long we stay. A public event that a teacher could've easily suggested we attend for extra credit.

"We'll be there," we said at the same time.

And then I told Mellie to go home, so I could make out with Rowan as a thank-you for saving her ass.

—Lise

March 13
Early morning
Dear Ms. Tilson,

It's 4 in the morning, and I can't sleep. My appointment with Lise's mom is tonight, and my mind is racing. My heart is trying to catch it, pounding a million miles a minute.

My cover story for my parents is that I'm going to the art show at the Empty Space. Lise's boyfriend Rowan's mom owns it.

It's so weird that Lise has a boyfriend. Okay, it's not weird; a lot of girls do. She doesn't talk about him much, so I kinda forget she has one. I guess when she and I are together, we're usually talking about me.

Rowan seems really nice. Like one of the good guys. I wonder if they've had sex. I wonder what it's like to have sex with someone you love. I can't even imagine it.

I can only think as far ahead as tonight.

I've never been to an art show. I want to go, to see how artists—real artists—create, but that's not the reason I'll be there tonight.

The plan is we'll go at seven, stay for an hour, and then Lise's mom's driver will pick us up around the corner from the gallery.

And, miracle of miracles, my parents okayed it.

I told them anyone who goes will get extra credit toward their final grade in your class, Ms. Tilson (I'm sorry I involved you in my scheme). My grades haven't been that great this semester, but my parents have been so busy with Dad's campaign they haven't paid much attention, and I think they may have even felt a little guilty about that. So they said yes to the art show without any fuss. The plan fell into place easily.

Too easily?

Nothing about this is easy. I have no idea what's going to happen tonight at the clinic. So maybe I'm owed something easy amid all of this hard stuff. But I can't help feeling like I'm being set up for a huge fall from something so high I'm going to break my neck.

I close my eyes.

I watch my life spiral out before me. I picture it so vividly that it feels like I'm there, living in that reality where I have HIS baby.

I open my eyes.

I'm not backing out.

Signed,
Mellie Rivers

March 13
Dear Ms. Tilson—

Tonight was the WORST night of my LIFE. Even worse than the day my parents told me they were getting divorced, because I could see that from ten miles away.

Tonight was filled with

so

much

PAIN.

And it wasn't even my pain. I can't stand it. I feel like I'm going to burst into a thousand fragments with the unfairness of it all. I want to scream so loud that I

bring

down

the night.

I did it. I ran out into my backyard and screamed so loud all the dogs in the neighborhood howled with me. My mom ran outside, yelling, "What's wrong?!" and I yowled in her face, tears streaming down my cheeks, and she knew. She knew why I was screaming into the darkness, and she joined me.

Sometimes I hate this world. Sometimes I think I'm not cut out to live in it. Sometimes I think I should go live off the grid in the mountains, foraging for food and writing manifestos about smashing the patriarchy.

But then I remember...as angry as I am, how much angrier must Mellie be? How much more unfair is it for her than for me? How much deeper must she want to escape, where no one can ever hurt her again?

I have to be strong. For her. For everyone like her who needs a friend to hold their hand while they live their worst nightmare coming true.

Maybe by doing that, I can make the earth a little less ugly.

—Lise

March 13
Maybe March 14
Still dark
Dear Ms. Tilson,

I was right.

No one can help me.

Lise tried, but she was wrong.

So much happened tonight that it's hard to think of it in the right order. My memory of the night is fragmented, sliced in pieces of before and after.

But I'm going to try to write down what I can.

I feel like I need to record it, that tonight was one of the nights you remember for the rest of your life, and I need to write it down so I don't forget.

I showed up at the Empty Space right at seven. This is the part of the night I want to remember the most. I want to remember how the art surrounded me, filled my senses so much that I could smell it. The artist had traveled across the country, taking photographs of places both forgotten and famous, like an abandoned silo in Iowa juxtaposed with Yellowstone. Then she'd printed the photographs and painted over them, so that each looked like a fantastical version of itself. The images were so vivid it was like I was *inside* the paintings, part of the art. You know how sometimes people say that art is experiential? I never understood that until tonight. I want to do that with my art, create something so powerful it makes someone have to sit down, as I did when I looked at the photograph/painting of the Big Sur coastline in California. The ocean, cliffs, and sky took my breath away. Someday I want to go there and paint it for myself.

So much happened between then and now. Even though I was at the gallery only a few hours ago, the experience of that art feels far away, like it's slipping from my fingers. I want to remember it. I *need* to remember it. Because maybe when this is all over, art will help save me.

I was the first one to arrive, so Rowan introduced me to his mom, Rosemary. He told her about my drawings, but I didn't have them with me, so Rosemary made me promise to come by to show them to her sometime. Lise showed up a little later, and we made small talk until more people arrived and Rowan's mom had to schmooze, and Rowan left to help pass out drinks. Then Lise and I slipped out the back door and hiked up the small hill behind the gallery to where a big black SUV with tinted windows was waiting for us.

"You're not the Mafia, are you?" I asked when I spotted the car.

Lise snorted. "Sometimes I wish we were. Then I wouldn't feel so vulnerable." She opened the door, but there was a car seat in the middle of the back seat, so Lise went around to the other side. I took a deep breath and climbed into the car. Lise strapped herself in. "Mellie, this is Daphne. She's my mom's driver."

Daphne twisted in the driver's seat and gave me a warm smile, revealing a deep dimple on her right cheek. "Hi, Mellie. Hey, Lise. Sorry I had to bring the baby. Dora's working late tonight."

My gaze dropped to the cherubic baby asleep in the car seat next to me. She had chubby cheeks that begged to be pinched and long dark lashes that rustled with each breath. "Oooh, I'm so glad you did!" Lise cooed and bent over the car seat. "Hi, Sadie," she whispered. "Is it sleepy sleepy-dreamy time?"

Daphne laughed and put the car in drive. "Not even Dora and I talk to her like that, Lise." She navigated the car off the back road and onto Main Street. I could see the Empty Space, bright and festive, with people holding wineglasses milling around on the sidewalk. Daphne took the first right turn away from the gallery and began to twist and turn through narrow back streets on our way to the clinic. I must have looked puzzled, because she made eye contact in the rearview mirror and said, "So no one follows us."

I nodded and looked over at Lise. She was still fawning over Sadie, stroking her cheek gently with one finger so she didn't wake her up. I finally looked down at the baby.

She was beautiful.

My heart twisted like a wet rag being wrung out to dry.

I couldn't stop myself. I reached out and touched the baby's hand. In her sleep, Sadie opened her fingers and curled them around mine, holding tight.

My breath caught in my throat. Lise looked at me. "It's okay," she whispered.

I shook my head. It was not okay. It would never be okay. "I want one," I whispered. "I want one, someday. Just not this one. Not now, not like this."

Lise didn't say anything, just reached across the car seat and took my other hand. I think she knew exactly how I felt. I was silent the rest of the ride, one hand in Lise's, the other hand in Sadie's. One hand desperately clutching my present, and the other hoping so hard for the future.

We passed the PCC and hot anger flared inside me. "Bitches," Lise said and flashed her middle finger at the building. We turned into the Whole Women's Health Clinic's parking lot. A big, white van was parked by the road. THE TRUTH MOBILE was painted across its side and big, gold angel wings sprouted from under the words. The back of the van was open, and a man was loading a couple of boxes and a few signs into it.

I stared out the window. "That's Henry Wickham. He goes to my church."

Lise groaned. "I call him You Could Die Tomorrow. He's here all day, every day, talking to women on their way into the clinic, telling them they could die tomorrow, so do they really want this blot on their soul when they meet their maker? He says the same thing to me when I escort." She squeezed my hand. "Don't worry, we're not going in the front."

As Daphne rounded the building, I turned back to watch Mr. Wickham. I had no idea this is where he spends his days. Does he have a job? I'm pretty sure his wife works. They have three kids, and I remember Mr. Wickham bragging to my father once that his wife has dinner on the table every day at 6:30. Does she support him financially and domestically so he can sit in front of the clinic and shame women all day long?

I didn't have time to wonder, as we'd arrived at the back of the building. It was very clever. It looked like we were turning off the street, but we were turning into a hidden alleyway behind the clinic that leads directly to a gated underground garage. Daphne swiped an access card, and the gate creaked open. I can sing for you the exact sound of that creak. It's imprinted in my brain.

Lise jumped out of the car when we stopped, but I couldn't move. Daphne helped me out of the car, then carefully unlatched the infant carrier seat. We all got onto the elevator. The silence was thick.

I turned to Daphne. "She's a beautiful baby."

Daphne looked at me. "You know what makes Sadie such a great baby?"

I raised an eyebrow. "What?"

"Because she was planned. She was wanted." She went on, waving her hand over her sleeping daughter, "Motherhood is the best job in the world. It's also the hardest job in the world. For sure, there are happy accidents. But if you're not ready for motherhood, it will drown you. Hell, it practically drowns you when you are ready for it." The elevator bumped to a stop on the second floor and dinged as the door opened. "You need to do what's right for you, and no one else can tell you what that is."

Daphne, carrying Sadie, and Lise both stepped off the elevator before me, leaving Daphne's words to sink in for a moment before I followed them. I'd seen firsthand how hard motherhood was. My mother never complains, but sometimes I wish she would. Sometimes I wish she would own up to just how hard of a job it is.

"Mellie."

I looked up. A petite woman with short black hair and gray-blue eyes standing just outside the elevator reached out to shake my hand. "I'm Alanna, Lise's mom. Come on in."

Inside, the clinic wasn't anything like I thought it would be. I guess I expected it to be cold and gray and dingy with bloodstains on the floor. That's the way my father makes it sound.

But it wasn't like that at all. The walls were a soothing green, and the carpet was plush and creamy. Cushy chairs lined the waiting room, with shabby chic end tables covered in magazines and books. A few large prints hung on the walls, one an art deco advertisement for perfume, another a 1950s ad for panty hose, and Rosie the Riveter, proclaiming "We Can Do It!"

Alanna opened the door next to the reception area and gestured for me to follow her. "I'm going to take you into an exam room, ask you some questions, and then we'll go from there. Okay?"

"Can Lise come?"

"Of course, if you want her to."

"I want her to." The instant I said it, Lise was next to me, in step with me and her mom.

"Daphne, can you wait?" Alanna asked.

"I'm good." Daphne set Sadie's carrier on the floor and settled in to the chair next to her.

We went through a set of doors behind the reception desk and into a long hallway with more doors leading off it. Here, the atmosphere was a little more sterile, a little more antiseptic, but pristine and comforting in its purity. Everything about this place said *We will care for you*.

It was a thousand times nicer than the PCC.

I wonder if anyone from the PCC has ever been there. I can't imagine they have, or they would've made their clinic better.

Alanna led me into the first exam room. There was a table covered with paper like any other doctor's office, but there were also two cushioned chairs and another art deco poster on the wall. "Where do you want me?"

"Anywhere you're comfortable," Alanna said.

I sat in one of the chairs and Lise sat in the other. Alanna sat on her rolling stool and wheeled herself close to us. "First, Mellie, I want to assure you that anything you say here is strictly confidential. You can tell me anything you feel comfortable sharing, and it will stay between you and me."

"Okay."

Alanna clipped a form onto a clipboard and pulled a pen out of her lab coat pocket. The first questions were easy—full name, date of birth, hospital I was born in, allergies. "First day of last period?"

"December eighth."

"Did you take a pregnancy test?"

"Yes."

"And it was positive?"

I nodded. She checked something on the form. "Have you been examined or had an ultrasound?"

I squeezed my eyes shut, the sound of the heartbeat still ringing in my ears. "Yes…at the PCC."

"You went to the PCC?" Alanna's eyes flashed, the same way that Lise's do when she gets riled up. "You don't have to elaborate. I know what goes on there." She shook her head. "I'm sorry you had to go through that." She scribbled something on the form, then set the clipboard and the pen on the counter. "Mellie, I need to ask you… Lise told me you were assaulted."

Assaulted. As if that's a better word than rape. I wanted her to just say it. RAPE. RAPE. RAPE. But I couldn't be mad at Alanna. She was simply doing her job, and she was being a lot more caring than those women at the PCC. I hunched my shoulders. "Yes," I said.

"Do you remember the date?"

"December twenty-first at three thirty in the afternoon," I said quietly.

Alanna leaned forward. "I'm so sorry that happened to you, Mellie."

Again, those words. They meant everything to me. It wasn't that I wanted people to feel sorry for me. I only wanted them to acknowledge that I was surviving something no one should ever have to experience. "It shouldn't happen to anyone," I said.

"No, it shouldn't," Alanna replied. She met my gaze. "It happened to me too. When I was in college."

My breath whistled in through my teeth. I looked at Lise. This was not a surprise for her. Like my mother's abortion, this was part of her family history. Except the way Lise's mom shared this, there wasn't any shame. They owned this history with power and truth. Slowly, I faced Alanna again. "You were raped?"

She nodded. "I was at a party. I'd had a lot to drink. A guy cornered me in the hallway, pushed me into an empty room." She shook her head. "I was too drunk or weak to fight him off. Not that I could've anyway, probably."

"Did you report it?"

"No. I didn't even know who he was, and I never saw him again." She clasped her hands together and flexed her fingers. "I have only one regret in this life, Mellie."

My stomach did a little flip-flop. "What is it?"

"That I spent even one minute thinking what happened to me was my fault."

Something broke inside me. I keeled forward, my head between my knees, my body shaking. Everything I'd shoved down, far away and out of sight, came to the surface, as if I'd finally been given permission to feel it all.

Because deep down, deep in my bones, I did think it was my fault.

Everything about December 21 is frozen in my mind, like a memory trapped inside a snow globe. I remember everything that happened before three thirty that afternoon. Helping Joanie get dressed, and changing her socks three times until she settled on the pink ones with rainbows. Playing Sorry! with my sisters. Baking Christmas cookies. Washing dishes. The news was on in the kitchen, reporting on the intern who's accused our president of raping her. "I can't wait until we get a woman in the White House," Bethany said to me. We were alone in the kitchen; she would never dare say this if my parents could hear. "We were talking about this in my government class. What would the country look like with a woman in charge?"

I'd thought about this too, secretly to myself. "Maybe men would finally respect women more," I said. "Maybe they'd realize there's more to us than just being mothers and wives." I turned away from the sink to put a clean cookie sheet on the rack to dry and caught sight of HIM in the doorway.

He didn't say anything, just gave me a grin that only covered half his mouth. I misread that grin. I thought he was privately agreeing with me. I thought he felt the same way, but he couldn't voice that opinion, not to our family, not in our circle. At three twenty-six, my mother sent me down to the basement to get the towels from the dryer. At three thirty, I learned the truth of that grin, and that a man can do anything he wants.

Now you know.

Just like Lise and Alanna.

I don't want to waste any more time blaming myself either. I have things to do. I have art to create. I have the Big Sur coastline to see. I have a life to live, and I am not going to give HIM one more minute of it.

In that moment, I replaced the deep-down-in-my-bones belief that what happened was my fault with another one: that I deserved a chance to take control of my life again. That terminating this pregnancy is the right thing to do.

As sure as my brain is not going to waste one more minute on HIM, neither is my body.

When I finally composed myself, Alanna went back into doctor mode and picked up my file. "So, here's the situation. You're fourteen weeks pregnant, since we calculate from the date of your last period rather than the exact date of conception. You have a lot of options at this point."

"I know which option I want," I said, and for the first time my voice sounded clear as I said it. "I want an abortion."

"Okay," Alanna said. "Colorado allows abortions up to thirty-six weeks, unlike other states that ban after twenty weeks, or even six weeks. But even so, your options are a bit more limited. You're too far along for a medical abortion, so you'd need to have a surgical one."

I felt my forehead furrow. "What does that mean?"

"If you weren't as far along, you could take a pill that would cause you to miscarry. A lot of women prefer that over surgery when it's an option. But you'd have to do it at home, which—"

"—is impossible," I said.

Alanna nodded. "It would be difficult to hide. There's a lot of bleeding and cramping, and it can go on for a few days. You'll still have some of that with a surgical abortion, but I think we could cover that better." She rubbed the bridge of her nose.

"But in order to schedule you for a surgical abortion, I need to do an ultrasound."

My whole body tensed.

Alanna put her hand on my knee. "I know what they probably did at the PCC. Our ultrasound machine here is much more sophisticated. For one thing, it's not vaginal. And I won't make you look. And"—she reached down into a cupboard below the counter next to her and pulled out a pair of huge, black, noise-canceling headphones—"you can wear these."

I stared at the headphones. "Is that—are you allowed to do that?"

A sly little look came over her face. "The law says I have to give you an ultrasound. It doesn't say you have to hear it." She handed me the headphones. "The law also says I have to tell you about the side effects of having an abortion. However, freedom of speech allows me to tell you that a lot of what the government makes me say is politically slanted and not true." She leaned in. "The risk of complications is very small. Surgical abortions are a very safe, very routine procedure. In fact, the chance of having complications that threaten your life later in a pregnancy are much greater than complications from a legal abortion." She pointed at the headphones. "Now put those on."

I'd never used noise-canceling headphones before. They really canceled *all* the noise. Even the noise in my head. I climbed on the table and leaned back while Alanna lifted my shirt and put cold, slimy jelly all over my stomach. I closed my eyes and the world became a blank slate. In that silence it was easy to imagine my life after this was over.

Lise held my hand the whole time.

I didn't ask her to, she just did it. After a while it felt like a natural extension of my arm. Me and Lise, connected. Her, here, for me.

When it was all done, and I was cleaned up, we sat back in the chairs. Alanna tapped the papers in my file into order and laid it on the counter. "Everything I see on the ultrasound indicates it's safe to terminate. It's your choice, Mellie. Do you want to go ahead with the surgical abortion?"

"Yes," I said. It was easier to say this time.

A glance passed between Alanna and Lise.

"The thing is," Alanna said, "because you're sixteen—"

"I know there's no parental permission law in Colorado," I said. "My dad talks about it, how we need to protect girls from making bad decisions for themselves."

"That's true." Alanna shifted in her chair. "You do not need your parents' permission to have the abortion. But…" She pinched the bridge of her nose. "There is a notification law. While you don't need their permission, I am required by law to tell your parents you are having an abortion forty-eight hours before you do it."

The air sucked out of the room.

I think the clock stopped ticking.

My world stopped.

I couldn't breathe.

"Can't you—?" It came out in a whisper. It sounded so far away, like it wasn't even my voice.

Alanna shook her head. "I can't make an exception. The state medical board could find out and shut down the clinic. You could get permission from a judge," she went on. "But we would have to get the process started now so you could meet with a judge as soon as possible."

Meet with a judge. I thought about all the judges my father has had over for dinner in the course of his campaign for state senate. Judges from all over his district and beyond. They're supposed to be apolitical, but based on the conversations I've overheard, they aren't. How could I expect them to grant my petition when they all know who my father is and what he stands for? "I can't meet with a judge," I said. The pitch in my voice was rising. "My parents will find out. I can't trust that they won't. My father is too connected."

"I'm so sorry, Mellie," Alanna said. "The closest state without any parental involvement laws is New Mexico. If we could get you to New Mexico—"

"How is that supposed to work?" I didn't mean it to come out so angry, not when these two amazing, kind people were trying so hard to figure this out for me. But I couldn't help it. I couldn't get to New Mexico. The only time I'd been allowed to go anywhere overnight without my parents was either to a sleepover at Delia's house or a church retreat. And I couldn't expect Delia to cover for me. Not now. Not for this.

All the strength I'd felt earlier seeped away, taken from me by the faceless men who'd all made this law, who'd sat in their oak-paneled room and judged teenage girls they didn't know anything about.

Except they weren't faceless.

They all wore one face.

My dad.

I pulled my hand away from Lise's. "I…I have to go. My parents…they'll expect me home."

"Mellie—"

"I don't know what I'm going to do," I said, answering the question that Alanna had left dangling. "I'm caught either way. I don't know what I'm going to do. I don't know what I'm going to do."

I ran down the hall, back to the waiting room where Daphne was nursing Sadie, singing to her. My insides twisted. She looked up as I flew across the room, opening her mouth to say something, but I was already out the front door before I heard what it was.

Outside, the night was dark and cold, the stars clear and

calm against everything that stormed inside me. The parking lot was empty now. The streets were deserted. I was truly alone. I looked up to the heavens. Once upon a time, the sky held limitless possibilities. Now it felt like it was closing in on me.

I wanted to scream.

I'm so sick of being afraid.

But I don't know what comes after the fear.

Signed,
Mellie Rivers

March 14
Close to dawn
Dear Ms. Tilson,

Years ago, before my dad started treating me like a "young lady," he took me and my brother hunting. I wasn't allowed to carry a gun, but I was allowed to hold and shoot my dad's when a deer appeared. I missed. Jeremy got super pissed at me because the gunshot startled the deer and all the other animals in the forest, so we didn't bring anything home. "Why'd you let her shoot?" he complained to my dad, whining that if he'd been given the chance, he wouldn't have missed and how we'd all be eating venison for the next two weeks.

Jeremy and I bickered for so long that my dad finally grabbed both our elbows and wheeled us back toward the car, saying he was sick of listening to us and we'd lost the privilege to hunt with him for the rest of the season. (I never got invited again.)

As we got closer to our car, a strange sound echoed through the trees. It was a high-pitched keen. We all froze. The sound rose and fell, like some kind of inhuman symphony. We followed it until we found a coyote caught in a bear trap. The lower part of its back leg was half torn off. Blood stained the leaves on the forest floor. The coyote keened again. Being so close, I could feel its pain, like its wail was coming from my own heart. As we approached, the coyote raised its head off the ground and stared at us with wide, brown eyes that were slowly dulling. Pushing us behind him with one hand, my dad raised his rifle with the other. One clean shot later, the coyote lay still and quiet.

I can't stop thinking about that coyote tonight. How the trap caught it and it lay there, dying, for who knows how long. I am that coyote. The jaws of that trap are around me now.

There is no way out.

New Mexico may as well be Neverland. If I have the abortion, my parents will know. If I don't have it, they will know. Either way, I'm caught with no escape.

I am not suicidal. I want my life. I want it so bad I can taste it on my tongue. *I want my life.*

I need a way out of the trap,

the one

clean

shot

that's going to put me out of my misery.

Signed,

Mellie Rivers

March 14

Dear Ms. Tilson—

I'm writing this before the second period bell. I haven't seen Mellie yet. I haven't seen her or talked to her since she ran out of the clinic last night. I wanted to call her, but she doesn't have a cell phone and I couldn't call her house. Not without raising suspicion. And I couldn't find her in the halls this morning. I'm worried about her. Cara cornered me as I passed by her locker in my search for Mellie. "Are you okay?" she asked. "You look weird."

"I am weird." I peered over her shoulder at the streams of kids moving past us in the hallway.

"No, I mean, more than usual. Lise. Lise." She snapped her fingers in front of my face and I looked at her. "You've been completely distracted lately. I don't mind you hanging out with other people, but I miss you. And you're making me worried."

I met her gaze and saw the real concern in the blue depths

of her eyes. I let out the breath I'd been holding all morning. "You're right, Cara. I'm sorry."

"You don't have to apologize, just tell me what's up."

"I can't."

She sighed overdramatically, and I put my hands on her shoulders. "I know that sucks, but it's all I've got right now. Let's just say...someone I care about needs my help. That's what's distracting me."

"Oh, Lise." She leaned her head so her cheek touched my hand that was on her shoulder. "Of course it is. That's who you are. That's why I love you."

Writing this now, I think if I was in Mellie's situation, I'd tell Cara what happened. I'd tell Rowan. I'd tell my mom. I'd be able to tell so many people and have their support and love.

But Mellie is all alone.

I have to see her today.

—Lise

March 14
Dear Ms. Tilson,

I didn't sleep at all last night, and this morning I had an idea. I went to the bathroom I share with my siblings and opened the medicine cabinet. *What's in here that I can use to get rid of this baby?* I thought.

Would half a bottle of aspirin do it? Laxatives? If I broke into my dad's liquor cabinet and drank an entire bottle of gin, would that do it? What would get rid of this baby without taking me down with it?

I stood in front of the medicine cabinet for so long that Bethany practically broke the door down banging on it and yelling for me to "Hurry up already!"

In the end, I swallowed a fistful of aspirin, a few expired prescription painkillers from when Hannah had her appendix out, half a bottle of cough syrup, and some Imodium, and then chugged two glasses of orange juice because the pamphlet from the PCC said too much vitamin C is bad for the fetus.

I was reaching for my coat when the first wave hit.

My bowels clenched. I dropped my coat and ran to the downstairs bathroom. "Are you okay?" Bethany called after me. I made it to the bathroom just in time. As I sat hunched on the toilet, my stomach churned upward. I grabbed the wastebasket and vomited into it. Bethany, who had followed me, backed out of the doorway. "Oh my God. Gross. Mom!"

"No, not Mom," I gasped in between the second and third wave of sick. But it was too late. A second later, my mother appeared. She waved Bethany away, telling her to get herself and the girls to school, and bent over me, rubbing my back and murmuring, like she did when I was little. I would've cried at her kindness if I hadn't been vomiting so hard. I wanted to curl into her, have her tell me I was going to be okay, even though I wasn't.

My insides were on fire, pain twisting its way up and down my intestines. Surely, surely, the baby was going to come out along with everything else inside me. But then my mother would see the blood and she'd know…

I shuddered. Mom pressed a cool washcloth to my forehead. "I'm going to replace this bag and I'll be right back," she said, whisking away the foul wastebasket. The instant she left, I reached out to shut the door behind her. I balled up a bunch of toilet paper to wipe myself, prepared to see blood.

There was no blood.

Just the brown and yellow stain of shit and piss.

I wiped again, so hard my skin burned. Not even a drop of red. Maybe it would take a while? Maybe it was still coming? But deep down I knew it wasn't. Deep down I knew there was no easy way out for me, no clean shot to put me out of my misery.

The door creaked open. "I called the school," Mom said, sliding the newly lined wastebasket in front of me. She was just in time too. She rubbed my back as I heaved. When I was done, she stepped back and appraised me. "Do you think it's something you ate?"

Thinking fast, I said, "There were crab cakes at that art opening last night. Maybe that."

"Oh, honey." Mom pushed a loose strand of my hair, dampened with sweat, behind my ear. "We live on a mountain in a landlocked state. You should know better than to eat crab."

"Thanks for the sympathy, Mom."

She laughed, a kind, generous laugh that she only let out when she wasn't doing a million things at once. My heart twisted with my gut. I missed that mother. I wanted the mother I could be truthful with, who I could ask what happened when she had her abortion, if it was really so horrible or if it was the best decision she ever made.

But I don't have that mother.

Lise has that mother.

I felt empty, my stomach only a dull ache and not a fiery pit of pain. "Give me a minute to clean myself up, okay?"

"I'll make you some tea." She took the dirty wastebasket and closed the door behind her.

I wiped myself one more time—still no blood—and flushed the toilet. I'd been so stupid, swallowing a bunch of pills that had no hope of aborting this baby. I was going to have to do it the hard way. I turned on the water in the sink and leaned against the cold porcelain, listening to the water run and run and run…at least I'd gotten out of school today. I wasn't sure I could face Lise. I couldn't be as strong as she wanted me to be, and I didn't want to see the disappointment in her eyes.

Mom asked me if I wanted to lie on the couch and watch TV or if I wanted to lie in bed with her iPad. We kids aren't allowed to have our own iPads, but sometimes Mom will let us borrow hers, like if we're out to dinner and Joanie starts to get whiny. I chose the iPad in bed.

Mom tucked me in up to my chin, placed a cup of tea on my nightstand, and put the wastebasket next to the bed. I was pretty sure I was all emptied out, my guts and my heart. My chest felt hollow.

"I have errands to run—will you be okay by yourself?"

"I think I'll be okay."

She gave me a sympathetic look. "Are you sure? There are some things I need to do for your dad's campaign but—"

"Mom, go. I'm fine." Both of us knew what we weren't saying: Dad's stuff was more important than a sick teenager.

"Okay. I'll be home around lunch."

I listened to her footsteps on the stairs, the creak of the closet door as she got her coat, the whoosh and slam of the front door as she left.

I'm writing this all alone. I have the entire house to myself. That *never* happens. It's too bad I'm too weak and nauseous to enjoy it.

Beneath the aftermath of the pills, I recognize the familiar nausea of morning sickness. It's still there, clinging to my insides, growing stronger inside me as I fade away.

Mom forgot to set the parental controls on the Netflix on her iPad, or she figured I'm a good girl who wouldn't watch anything she disapproves of. And sure, I'm going to watch as many episodes of *Parks and Recreation* as I can before she gets home, because Dad has never approved; he thinks Leslie Knope is far too liberal. But first there's something else I need to look up on the internet. It's a good thing I overheard Dean Frasier telling Jess Niles how to wipe your search history clean in French class recently. He didn't want his parents to find out he searched for gay porn. Apparently Jess Niles is allowed to have an iPad, even if his parents have no idea he's gay.

Oh—please don't share that. I don't want to be responsible for outing him.

I wonder how many other kids at school are living double lives and hiding secrets from their parents.

Signed,
Mellie Rivers

March 14

Dear Ms. Tilson—

I'm really, really worried about Mellie.

She wasn't in school today (which you know since she wasn't in class). I should've called her last night after the clinic, made up something to get her on the phone. But I figured I'd see her in school, and we could figure out together what she's going to do.

But she wasn't here. I have no idea what is in her mind, and I am so worried, Ms. Tilson, so freaking worried.

So I went to her house.

I think I went to her house once, a long time ago when we were kids. I didn't remember it until I was standing at the top of her driveway. Suddenly I had this sharp feeling I had been there before. It must've been in the winter, because I remember snow. I remember sledding down the hill from the top of the drive toward the house. And I remember her mother having hot chocolate for us when we came inside, red-cheeked and covered in snow, laughing.

I wish I could take us back to that day and warn Mellie about what would happen, give her some other destiny to avoid all this pain.

I descended the driveway, practicing what I was going to say with every step. *I'm dropping off Mellie's homework, Mrs. Rivers. Is she here? I'd love to see her.* By the time I got to the front door, I was shaking. It didn't help that the door is *huge.* It belongs on a castle in England, not on a house in Colorado. It's made out of heavy, dark wood, and you can totally imagine it at the mouth of a dungeon. No wonder she can't tell her parents.

I rang the doorbell, hoping Mellie would answer. The English dungeon door creaked open. No such luck.

"Hi, Mrs. Rivers," I said.

She squinted at me. "Hello, uh—"

"Lise," I supplied. "Lise Grant. I'm a friend of Mellie's from school. I...I used to be in Girl Scouts with her."

"Oh, yes. Hello." She pressed her lips together, maybe recalling the reason Mellie left Girl Scouts. I rushed on so she didn't have too much time to think about it.

"Is Mellie here? I have her homework assignment from biology."

"How thoughtful of you." She pushed the English dungeon

door open a little wider to allow me to step in. "She's upstairs in her room."

"Is she okay?"

"She's better now. I think she ate some bad crab last night at that art show." She said "art show" like it was a euphemism for "biker bar" or something.

"That's too bad."

"Were you there?"

"Um—yes. My boyfriend's mother owns the gallery."

"Your boyfriend." Again, she said "boyfriend" as though what she was really saying was "the man you dance naked for at a strip club."

"I didn't eat the crab," I said quickly, because I knew that wasn't why Mellie was sick.

"Well, Mellie shouldn't have either," Mrs. Rivers said. "But she's feeling better now. Go on up."

"Thanks."

I'm going to pause here and say: I haven't seen Mrs. Rivers in a really long time—not up close, anyway; I've seen her around town and in the paper. But back when Mellie and I were friends before, she didn't seem like the kind of mother who would blame her daughter for getting food poisoning.

And if she could blame Mellie for that, I can only imagine what she would do if she found out Mellie was pregnant. Even if she'd been raped.

What I'm trying to say is, I began to understand why Mellie can't tell her parents. I didn't quite get it before. I tell my mom everything. I don't know how to live in a world where I couldn't do that.

I glimpsed Mellie's two youngest sisters on my way to the stairs, doing their homework at the dining room table. The radio was on, snippets of a religious show wafting out through the house. At least, I assumed it was a religious show because I heard *Jesus* and *Lord* and *Bible* a lot in the time it took me to get from the front door to the stairs.

Memory is a funny thing. Even though I was only in this house once or twice, I knew to turn left at the top of the stairs and to go all the way down the hall. Mellie's door was half closed. I knocked and pushed it open. Mellie looked up at me from her bed where she was covered in blankets. Her cheeks were pale and her eyes overbright. "What are you doing here?"

"Bringing you your biology homework," I said and closed the door behind me. I crossed to her bed and perched on it. Mellie didn't make any room for me. She did not look happy to see me. In fact, she looked mad. Really mad.

"Are you kidding, Lise? This was a bad idea." She glanced to the door and lowered her voice. "They're going to get suspicious."

"I don't think your mom suspected anything."

"But now she will." Mellie ran her hand over her face. "Lise, you don't think. You have no idea."

My insides got all twisted, seeing her in that bed. She looked small and alone. No matter how much I try to be there for her, she really is all by herself in this. She's the one that has to go through it. I can't carry that weight for her.

"Mellie." I put my hand on her arm and felt her stiffen. "I'm really sorry about last night. I should've told you about the law. I just...I thought it would be better coming from my mom, but the truth is I was chickenshit."

She narrowed her eyes at me. "You're not chickenshit. You are the opposite of chickenshit." She pulled the blankets tight up under her chin. "But you shouldn't have come here. I can't give them any reason to watch me more closely than they already do."

"What are you going to do?" I asked in a low voice.

She didn't answer, and turned her head to look out the window. I followed her gaze. Twilight had fallen outside. One star was visible in the darkening sky. *I wish I may, I wish I might, first star I see tonight...* I wish for Mellie to be okay. For her to come through this. If not unscathed, then with scars that would eventually fade.

"I'll figure it out," she said, but she still wasn't looking at me.

The bedroom door banged open. I stood. Mellie's sister Bethany flung her backpack onto the other bed and stared at me, her hands on her hips. "Oh, hey. Lise, right?"

"Yeah...hi. I was dropping off Mellie's homework."

Bethany wrinkled her nose and peered around me. "How are you feeling, Mellie?"

"Okay. Better."

"Good. Don't want you fouling up our bathroom."

"Bethany."

"Well, it was gross. Like, I was nauseous all day thinking about it." Bethany opened her eyes wide, a grin licking at the corners of her mouth. "It was coming out both ends."

"BETHANY! SHUT UP!"

I would've laughed at this little sisterly interplay, but my mind was too busy whirring, ticking, clicking the details into place. Coming out both ends? Yes, *gross*…but also not morning sickness. And I knew it wasn't the crab because I *had* eaten the crab last night and I was fine. And so was Rowan.

I looked down at Mellie, who met my gaze for an instant before turning away again. And I knew. Oh God, I knew. She'd taken something. She'd tried to abort the baby on her own. What kind of dangerous cocktail had she ingested? Whatever it was, it could've been way, way worse.

But I couldn't say anything because Bethany was there, chattering on about school and how annoying her friends were, and all I could do was stare at Mellie.

"…didn't know you and Mellie were such good friends."

I became aware of the silence as Bethany waited for me to respond. "What? Oh, sure. We have some classes together. I didn't want Mellie to get behind." I dug into my bag and pulled out the assignment pages for the biology homework. "In fact, Mrs. Snyder went over something in class that's not in the book so I'll jot it down on the back here." I scribbled the first thing that popped into my brain, a note that hopefully no one else would see. "I guess I should go," I said, putting the paper—scribble side down—on Mellie's nightstand. "I hope you feel better."

"Thanks, Lise."

"Bye, Lise!" Bethany said in a cheery voice that I honestly couldn't tell was real or fake.

I backed out of the room, hurried downstairs, and was almost at the English dungeon door when it suddenly opened. I slid to a halt.

"Who are you?" Mr. Rivers demanded when he saw me standing in his house.

I wish I could say I stood tall and filled the space as much as he did. I wish I could tell you that I told him off for his misogynistic politics, or that I hoped his Democratic opponent beat him in the state senate race, or that he should care about his family more than his political office. All that stuff *was* running through my head, but I could only stammer out, "L-Lise Grant. I…I'm a friend of Mellie's."

"She was bringing Mellie her homework, dear." Mrs. Rivers materialized behind me and walked over to peck her husband on the cheek. "Mellie was home sick today."

"Is she okay?"

"She had a touch of food poisoning. Some bad crab from that art show she went to last night."

Mr. Rivers shook his head. "I told her it was silly to go in the first place."

"She'll be fine." Mrs. Rivers helped him off with his coat and hung it in the closet by the door. "Dinner's in fifteen minutes."

"Good," he said, checking his watch.

I ducked around him without a word and was almost out the door when he turned. "Grant, you said?"

So. Freaking. Close. "Uh, yes. Lise Grant."

His eyes narrowed. "I don't think I know your family. What church do you go to?"

"We go to the Universalist Church sometimes."

"Oh." He said it like a long, drawn-out vowel that had more subtext than a Shakespearean play. "You're one of those families."

Those families? What the hell did that mean? Heat balled up inside me. "Yes, sir," I said. "We're one of those families who believe that everyone is equal, that love is love, and that God doesn't belong to just one religion." I didn't wait for him to respond, just turned on my heel and slammed that English dungeon door behind me.

MY GOD, it felt good to do that. To say that to him. To them.

But now I'm worried my act of defiance is going to bring Mellie more questions, more scrutiny.

Which is exactly what she doesn't need.

—Lise

March 14
Night
Dear Ms. Tilson,

DAMN LISE GRANT AND HER DAMN MEDDLING.

She stopped by the house today, saying she was dropping off homework. Which was so stupid because, hello, everyone gets homework online nowadays. What the hell was she thinking? She wasn't. She was meddling. And now I'm screwed.

Apparently she said something rude to Mom and Dad on her way out. They didn't say what, but I can only imagine. The instant she left, they came up to my room to grill me about her. Their rapid-fire questions made me feel like I was in front of a firing squad.

How do you know her?

Are you friends with her? Why haven't we heard you mention her?

What's going on with you and Delia? Why hasn't she come around lately? What was your fight about?

What does Lise's father do?

Her parents are divorced?

Why did they get divorced?

Where does her father live?

Who is this boyfriend of hers?

Did you go to the art show with her last night? Whose idea was it?

Their interrogation ended with, "We think this Lise is a bad influence. You should make things right with Delia."

Mom said I didn't have to come to dinner because my stomach was still upset, and brought me some tea and toast to eat in my room. Before she left, she gave me this appraising look, like, was I really sick? Was I faking it? What had happened to her perfect daughter with her perfect friends? I could see it in her eyes. Doubt. Distrust. Suspicion.

And that's all Lise's fault.

Alone in my room, I pushed away the toast and took a sip of tea. When I put the mug on the nightstand, a little spilled onto the homework assignment Lise had left. It spread across the paper, staining it light brown, and bleeding through to Lise's scribbled writing on the other side. I snatched the paper and turned it over.

Don't do anything stupid.

I'll help you figure this out.

My stomach flipped. I folded the paper into quarters and

tucked it into this journal, the only safe place I know no one will look. Damn her. How will she help me figure this out? Is she going to get me to New Mexico undetected for two days? Will she get me permission from a judge in the next week to have an abortion without my parents being notified? Will she convince her mother to break the law and not tell? No. She can't do any of those things.

Whatever. I've already figured out what I'm going to do. I just have to line it all up. Then everything will be okay.

I know Lise means well, but she can't help me now. I can't risk her getting me found out. I can't trust her anymore.

Signed,
Mellie Rivers

March 15
Dear Ms. Tilson—

I'm back to stalking Mellie. She's not speaking to me, so I have no choice. I tried to apologize for going to her house, but she brushed me off. I asked her to meet me in the bathroom after school, and even though she said no, I still went, hoping she would show up. She didn't.

Today I backed off and didn't try to talk to her. Let her come to me. I barely saw her all day. When I did, she seemed paler and more withdrawn. She's still not speaking to Delia. I don't think I saw her talk to anyone all day.

Look, I know spying on someone is not cool, but I am so worried about her. She's desperate. I told Mom why I think Mellie was home sick, but she says we can't force her to come back to the clinic. The whole point of the right to choose is that Mellie has the right to choose whatever she wants to do, Mom says. Sometimes I really hate it when Mom is all noble like that.

After school I hung around just inside the library, hoping that she'd come and we could talk in the make-out nook. After a long time, way past when all the other kids were at after-school clubs or in the library studying, I saw her come out of the bathroom near the office. She walked right past the library, toward the front entrance. After she'd gone through the doors, I stepped out of the library and followed her.

She went left when her house is to the right. I waited near a tree in case she turned around. She didn't. She went to the pay phone on the corner, the same phone I saw her at when I first started following her. Today she made a phone call that lasted several minutes. Her back was to me so I couldn't see her face as she talked.

God, I hope she wasn't calling the PCC.

After she hung up, she crossed the street and walked up Cedar Avenue until she disappeared from my view. I traced her route, far enough behind so that by the time I saw her again, she was finishing up at the ATM outside of the bank. Then she walked another block and turned on Crestview, which I knew meant she was heading home.

It all could've been nothing. She doesn't have a cell phone, so maybe she was calling home to tell them she was on her way. I have my own account at the bank too, so I use the ATM all the time. It could've been completely innocuous. But knowing her situation, my gut tells me it wasn't.

I was too jumpy to go home, so I went to the art gallery. Rowan works there on Monday afternoons, so I hung out with him. It was quiet—it usually is on weekdays—so we did our homework and wrote each other silly notes. On any other day, it would've made me so happy. I would've danced home and sang while cooking dinner, giggling to myself over his charming little verses. Today's winner:

Don't sell me a lime

It will sour the sweet taste

Of your love's cocktail.

Instead, I was quiet and preoccupied, even in the face of Rowan's love poems. And he let me be that way. He knows I'm still chasing this problem and that it's better to let me brood than to pester me with questions. He only said, "If you want to talk, I'll listen."

"Just keep writing me poems," I told him. What I wanted to say was, I wish I could tell you because I know you would listen. You would be compassionate and empathetic; you would stroke my palm and tell me I was a good person.

But I can't. And deep down, I know I don't deserve that praise. If I was a good person, Mellie would still be talking to me, and I wouldn't be following her through town like some pathetic shadow of a friend.

Okay, you know what? I'm going to spend exactly one night—tonight—feeling helpless and useless. I'm going to make myself a hot chocolate using whole milk instead of water, and eat an entire column of Oreos, not the suggested serving size of two. I'm going to watch *Parks and Recreation* on Netflix, and I'm going to give myself a pedicure. Then tomorrow I'm going to put on my big-girl panties and figure out how to help Mellie.

—Lise

March 19

Dear Ms. Tilson—

I cornered Mellie in the girls' locker room before gym class. Everyone else was filing into the gym, but I caught her arm and pulled her back. "Tell me what's going on in your head," I said.

"My parents were all over me this weekend thanks to you," she said, yanking her arm out of my grasp. "I don't need that, Lise. You're making things worse for me, not better."

"I'm sorry," I said. "I really, really am. I only want to help."

"Well, you're not. And you can't."

"Mellie." I jumped in front of her so she couldn't go through the door. "What are you going to do?"

"It's none of your business. Get out of my way before we're marked late."

I didn't move. "Mellie, please don't do anything stupid."

"I'm not." But she wouldn't look at me when she said it.

"You took something the other day. I know you did.

Please—don't do anything like that. You have no idea what could happen."

Then she did look at me, right in the eyes. "Maybe not, but I know what will happen if my parents find out. I'll take my chances."

Before I could stop her, she pushed past me into the gym.

Ms. Tilson, I'm scared of what she's going to do to herself.

—Lise

March 21

Dear Ms. Tilson,

I know it was stupid, but I didn't know what else to do.

I got the number off a website I found when I searched on Mom's iPad. If he had a website, that meant he was somewhat legit. That's what I told myself, even though I knew I was lying. I had a squelchy, squishy feeling in my stomach, but I shoved it down. This was the only way to do it so my parents wouldn't know.

When I called the phone number, the guy who answered had a hoarse, scratchy voice, like he'd just woken up. "It's $500 cash."

"I have it," I whispered into the pay phone. The same pay phone that I used to call RAINN, that I used to call the PCC. That pay phone knows all my secrets.

He gave me an address. It was in Pinecrest, thirty miles away. I'd never been to Pinecrest. My dad had a campaign stop there once, but my mother said there was no way she was bringing us there with him, that it wasn't safe. It's one of the only times she's said no to him. I tried not to think about what she'd say about me going there—especially if she knew what I was going there to do.

I took extra money out of the bank for a cab to take me there. The man told me to come in the late afternoon, and it wasn't until second period this morning that I realized I'd forgotten to make an excuse for my parents. I gasped and sat straight up in French.

"*Oui*, Mademoiselle Rivers?" Mrs. Landen—sorry, Madame Landen—asked me. Suddenly all the eyes in the room were on me. I shrank down in my seat and shook my head.

"*Je suis désolé*," I murmured. "Nothing."

Shit, shit, shit—sorry, *merde, merde, merde*. I thought the rest of the period, my mind racing over reasons I might be away for at least three hours, but I dismissed one after another for being too see-through or too implausible.

When the bell rang, I packed up my French book and pushed out of my seat, backing right into Susanna. A few weeks ago, Susanna and I would've laughed about this, and it would've been no big deal, given that we've been friends since we were five. Except now she's one of Delia's minions.

"I'm really sorry," I said, my eyes on the floor. "It was an accident."

"No worries," Susanna said. When I looked up, she was smiling at me. *Smiling.* "How are you, Mellie?"

"Okay, I guess." I went to move past her, but she hooked her arm in mine and propelled us both toward the door.

"Look, I think Delia's being an idiot," she said. "I miss hanging out."

Suddenly, Susanna was a sunflower growing in a field of snow. "I miss hanging out too," I admitted. "Honestly, I don't know what I did to get Delia so mad at me."

"Personally, I think she's jealous about Hannah and Brandon's wedding. The world isn't currently revolving around her, and she hates that."

I forced a laugh even though my insides were churning.

We had reached the hallway. Susanna squeezed my arm before she let go. "Call me if you want to hang out—you know, without Delia. Or if you need to talk. I bet your house isn't too fun between your dad's campaign and the wedding. I can tell it's stressing you out."

I stared at her. "You can?"

"Well, sure." She leaned toward me. "No offense, but you've got bags under your eyes. And I bet Delia freezing you out isn't helping matters."

"No. No, it's not." Before I could think the better of it, I said, "Actually, can I ask you a favor? You'd be helping me out."

Susanna raised an eyebrow. "What?"

"I need a few hours this afternoon…to…um…do some secret bridal shower stuff. Not even my mom knows about it because it's sort of a surprise for her too…so I don't want them to know what I'm up to, but I don't—"

"You need me to cover for you?" She grinned. "Sure. No problem."

"Really?"

"Yeah, we'll say you're hanging out at my house. Do you need me to drop you somewhere?" Susanna was the only girl in my old circle who had her own car. Probably because she was an only child.

I couldn't believe my luck. "Would you drop me at Mountainside Plaza?" There were always cabs waiting there to drive shoppers home. I gave Susanna a tight, quick hug. "Thank you. You're a lifesaver."

She had no idea.

I didn't even have to lie to Bethany when I told her I was hanging out with Susanna after school. I waved to her from Susanna's car as we drove away from the school. Susanna was cheery and funny the whole ride to Mountainside. When we pulled into the parking lot, she put the car into park and twisted in her seat toward me. "Are you okay, Mellie?"

I swept my gaze across the line of stores. A few cabs were idling by the curb. Now that we were here, my stomach tightened. "I'm fine," I said. I think my voice shook. "Why?"

"You just seem—"

"I know, I know. I'm stressed."

"No." Something in her voice made me catch her eye in the rearview mirror. "It's more than stress. It's…sadness."

She saw it. She saw me. She saw what Lise had seen, what Delia was too self-centered to notice. I took a deep breath. I wanted to tell her and ask her to drive me to Pinecrest, hold my hand while this anonymous guy gave me an abortion. I searched her face, the words hanging on the tip of my tongue, ready to spill out…

Something glinted in the corner of my eye.

Dangling from her rearview mirror was a burnished gold crucifix with Jesus Is The Way etched across the bottom below his nailed feet. It had been there the whole drive, of course, but I hadn't noticed until the sun had caught it just right. Reminding me. Warning me. Susanna had helped me, but she wasn't safe. I couldn't trust her. Not with this.

I cleared my throat. "You're so sweet for worrying about me," I said in a voice that sounded like my mother's. "I'm fine. It's been a bit of a rough time, that's all." I didn't wait for her reaction. I opened the car door and slid out. "Thanks for the ride!"

Susanna waved and backed out of the parking spot. I watched until she had turned back onto the main road and was out of sight before I walked over to the row of cabs. The first one wouldn't take me to Pinecrest. The second one quoted me a fare that seemed outrageous. The third cabbie was a woman. "Sure, honey, hop in."

I wondered if I told this woman why I was going to this particular address, would she wait for me, make sure I got home okay? Would this stranger take care of me?

But she didn't ask why I was going to Pinecrest, and I didn't offer a reason.

When we finally got there, the sun had dropped low, the light stretching pink and orange across the snow-tipped mountains. The cabbie rolled to a stop next to a bent metal sign that read PINECREST MOBILE PARK. The *o* in Mobile had been shot out and was now a ring of bullet holes.

The cabbie peered out her front window. "Um…"

"It's okay," I said, forcing brightness into my tone. "My cousin lives here. I visit all the time."

She shrugged, still skeptical, but I gave her a pretty nice tip and she didn't say anything else. I marched away from the cab like I knew exactly where I was going, and heard the tires crunch as she drove away. I dug out the paper with the address from my pocket. Unit E-32. I'd assumed that was an apartment number, or an office suite, not a lot in a trailer park. My insides twisted up tight. But then I thought about Alanna calling my parents. I thought about my parents finding out about the baby, about the abortion…the abortion they would surely put a stop to if they found out forty-eight hours ahead of time. Maybe they would lock me in the house until I went into labor.

I put one foot in front of the other, until I came to row E. The park was quiet in the lengthening shadows. I thought I saw a couple of people peek out their windows at me, but they disappeared as soon as I caught sight of them. The air smelled weird, like a mix of cooking and something else I couldn't quite place. Something that smelled like…chemistry class? When I got to lot E-32, I headed toward the trailer. Before I even got to the door, it opened.

"Come on, get in," a voice whispered at me.

The light inside was dim. All the curtains in the trailer were drawn shut so that there was no natural light. When the guy stepped back from the door, it was the first time I saw his face. He was thin and wiry with a thick beard that I think was less intentional than just a laziness about shaving.

"Do you have the money?"

I nodded and dug it out of my backpack. He took it from me before I held it out and counted it. "Good." He pointed to a door at the back of the trailer. "Take everything off from the waist down and lie on the bed."

"O-okay."

But I couldn't get myself to move. My limbs had gone cold. My heart, my brain, every organ in my body shouted *This Is Not*

Okay. I thought about the comfort and cleanliness of Alanna's clinic. But she will tell your parents, I reminded myself. I forced my legs to move and my heart pounded louder with every step I took toward the bedroom.

Someone banged on the trailer door. I shrank against the wall as the guy pulled it open. "Not now," he growled.

"Hey man, I got money this time."

"I said, not now, I'm busy."

"But I need it—"

"Come back later." The guy slammed the door. Whoever was outside tapped on the door again, but the guy shook his head. "Douchebag," he muttered and headed toward me.

I ducked into the bedroom. On the wall over the bed was a framed diploma from the University of Minnesota Medical School. It was for Kyle Jameson, which I assumed was this guy's name. I felt him come into the room behind me and turned. "You went to medical school?"

"Of course I went to medical school. I'm a fucking doctor."

"Oh…I just…I didn't know. You're a licensed doctor?"

"Yes," he said, going to a table in the corner where I saw various medical tools laid out. They seemed clean enough, even if the rest of the room didn't look sterile like Alanna's clinic. I stood in front of the bed with my hands clawed around the waistband of my pants. "Are you gonna stand there or do you want to get this over with?" Kyle asked over his shoulder.

Yes, I wanted to get it over with. But everything about this screamed WRONG. But if I was going to keep this a secret, I didn't see another choice. I couldn't do it the right way. After all, women had done worse in the days before *Roe v. Wade*, hadn't they? I slid off my pants. They pooled on the floor at my feet.

Kyle faced me, holding an instrument shaped like a hook. "I don't have all day. Take off your underwear and lie back on the bed. Spread your legs like a butterfly."

My whole body froze, my breath shallow, in and out, in and out. *Spread your fucking legs.* HE had said that. In the basement.

Kyle stared at me. "Do you want to do this or not?"

A slant of dying sunlight through the drawn curtains gleamed off the silver hook in his hand. "I—"

"You won't get your money back."

"I know, I just—"

Someone pounded on the door again. The whole trailer shook. "Jesus Christ," Kyle muttered. "I said, come back later," he yelled. There was silence for a second, and then—

"MELLIE!"

I started, my body coming unfrozen.

"MELLIE!"

"What the fuck?" Kyle pointed the hook at me. "I told you to come alone."

"I did!"

"MELLIE! LET ME IN!"

"Then who the fuck is that?"

"She—" *She came to rescue me.*

There was more banging on the door. "Goddammit." Kyle strode out of the bedroom, the hooked tool still in his hand. I jerked on my pants before following him. The chemical smell was stronger now, burning the inside of my nostrils. Kyle wrenched open the door.

Standing there, like a lantern against the darkness, was Lise. She was breathing hard, her fist raised high to bang on the door again. She looked past Kyle and saw me, barefoot in the middle of Kyle's trailer. I couldn't meet her eyes. "Mellie, please don't do this."

"I don't have a choice," I whispered.

She took a step inside the trailer. "I know it feels like that," she said. The tenderness in her voice made me want to cry. I didn't deserve it, not after how I ran out on her and her mom. "But this isn't the right way to do it. It's not safe."

"Who the fuck do you think you are?" Kyle blocked Lise from getting any deeper into the trailer.

"I'm her friend, and I'm taking her home," Lise said. I couldn't believe how calm she was. "I can see the rust on your scalpel from here. How many women have you used that on? What the hell do you think you're doing?"

"I'm helping women who need it," Kyle shot back at her. "It's not my fault this country has some backward-ass abortion laws."

"You're right," Lise agreed. "But you could help to change those laws, instead of taking advantage of women in a vulnerable situation. You're despicable."

Kyle pointed the hook at her again, first at Lise and then at me. "You're not getting your money back, you know."

"Actually, she is, or I'm reporting you to the police."

Kyle swung the hook back at Lise, inches from her face, but his eyes flitted toward the bedroom. Oh, God. Did he have a gun in there?

Lise eased away from the hook and reached out to me. "I have a car waiting at the entrance," she said, looking at Kyle. "I told the driver that if I'm not back in fifteen minutes to call the police." She glanced at her watch. "You've got about six minutes, and it'll take us nearly that long to walk back. So by all means, let's fight more about the money."

"Fine," Kyle said through gritted teeth, jerking his head at the kitchen table where he'd left my money. I grabbed it, my coat, and my bag. As we moved to the door, Kyle punched the wall. "You two are real bitches, you know that?"

Lise laughed. She actually laughed. I was shaking with fear, but she *laughed*. "That's right. We're nasty women, and don't you forget it," she said, and pulled me outside.

Darkness stretched wide over us. There were no streetlights, only shadows and distant starlight. Still holding my hand, Lise led me through the maze of mobile homes, their doors and windows shut tight against us. The chemical stench still hung in the air.

"God, what is that smell?" I said as we hurried.

"Meth," Lise said. "This town is full of meth labs. That guy—he was a dealer."

I shuddered, clutching Lise's hand harder. This was why my mother wouldn't take any of us to Pinecrest. "Come on," Lise said and we took off running, our footsteps pounding as hard and fast as my heart.

The big black SUV sat waiting for us. Lise opened the door and pushed me inside. Daphne twisted in the driver's seat. "Are you okay?"

"She hadn't done it yet."

"Thank God." She put the car in drive and peeled onto the road. I watched the dim lights of the mobile park grow fainter until it was a shadow.

And then everything that had been twisted up inside me unwound. I tipped sideways in my seat and curled into a fetal position, my whole body trembling. Lise gently eased my head onto her lap and stroked my hair. "It's gonna be okay," she murmured. "We'll figure it out. We'll figure it out."

Not once did she tell me how stupid I'd been. Not once did

she go through any of the what-ifs that could have happened. She didn't even tell me how she knew where I was.

She just stroked my hair.

I will never not trust her ever again.

Signed,
Mellie Rivers

March 21
Dear Ms. Tilson—

How could Mellie be so stupid?! Doesn't she know what could've happened? She could've DIED. It might sound dramatic, but it is true. Do you know how many women died before *Roe v. Wade*? *Countless.* Literally. We can't count them because their deaths were usually recorded as something vague, like sepsis or an infection. I can't even tell you how many women my mother sees who tried to do what Mellie was going to do, but the procedure got botched and Mom has to fix them. Nowadays it's usually with pills they ordered online from Mexico or something they pulled out of their medicine cabinet. Once, my mom said a woman called the clinic because she was too far away to get there, or to any clinic, and she said, "Here's what I have in my house…why don't you just tell me what I can use to get rid of it?" That night was one of the only times my mother came home from work and cried.

That's what some people don't understand. The country can make abortions illegal or harder to get, but it won't stop women from getting them. Abortions will only get more dangerous and more women will die. One of those women could've been Mellie.

I wanted to shake her and tell her what an idiot she was… but I couldn't. Because I get it. She thought it was her only way out. And I get that it's the only way for her to get both things she wants: an abortion and for her parents to never know. Because she can't do both legally. Not in this state, anyway.

God, you should've seen her. Crumpled in my lap on the car ride home. I couldn't tell her how stupid she was, not while she was crying like that. I could feel her heart breaking, right there in my lap. I thought getting her out of that horrible place would be enough, but it wasn't. It won't be. There's still a huge black cloud of a problem that I can't fix.

About ten miles outside of Wolverton, Mellie wiped her cheeks, sniffled, and sat up. "How did you know?"

"How did I know what?"

"Where I was. What I was doing."

"I figured out you were trying to get rid of it on your own after you took all those pills the other day."

"How did you know *that*?"

"Mellie. I volunteer at the clinic. I hear a lot."

She pressed her lips together. "I should've known it wouldn't fool you. But still. How did you find me in Pinecrest?"

I cleared my throat and dug into the seat pouch in front of me for the bottle of water Daphne always keeps stocked there. Mellie watched me take a long drink with her eyebrows raised. When I put the bottle down and I still hadn't answered, she said, "Lise."

"Okay, fine. I did a little digging."

"You stalked me again."

"I didn't stalk—I went online and figured you'd go to the first website that popped up. I called the guy and pretended I needed an abortion too, so I got the address. And then..." I trailed off because it really did sound like something a stalker would do. I mean, this was Lifetime Movie territory.

"And then you followed me to Mountainside Plaza, saw me get out of Susanna's car and into the cab, called Daphne, and told her to follow me. Right?"

"Wow," I said. "That was eerie."

"*Lise.*" She glared at me for a moment, her mouth all scrunched up like she was revving up to get really loud and angry. Instead, she grabbed my arm and pulled me into a tight hug. "Thank you," she said. "Thank you for getting me out of there. It wasn't the right thing to do."

Yeah, understatement of the year, but I didn't say so. I hugged her back. I felt her start to crumble again. I hugged her tighter. "We'll figure it out," I said again.

"How? Your mom has to tell my parents."

"Well," I said, my words delicate, "would that be the worst thing?"

Mellie pulled back with a sharp intake of breath. "Yes. Yes, it would."

"Why? It wasn't your fault. You are the victim here."

She shook her head. "They won't see it that way."

I wanted to think she was wrong, but I know many women get blamed for their own rapes. *What were you wearing? How much did you have to drink? Why were you walking to your car alone?* It's so easy to blame women that even other women do it without thinking. Still…these were her parents. "If anyone is going to take your side, it should be your parents. Right?"

A red splotch spread across Mellie's throat as she swallowed hard. "It must be nice to have parents that you never doubt are on your side," she whispered. "I don't have that." A tear leaked out of the corner of her eye and spilled down her cheek, leaving a long trail in its wake. My own throat tightened. I did have that. I told myself to hug my mom tight and thank her when I got home.

"Plus," she added, "it's more complicated than that." She stared out the window.

I knew she was talking about the guy who raped her, and I wondered for the millionth-and-one time who it was. I wish I knew so I could go all Arya Stark on him. I blew a hard breath out. "Well, my mom has to tell them. I don't think we're getting around that. So, what will they do when they find out?"

Mellie turned back to me. "They'll stop me from having the abortion."

"You mean, you think they'll physically stop you?"

"Yes," Mellie said without a trace of doubt in her voice. "They will lock me in my room. They will block the door. I'm not being overdramatic, Lise. They will do everything they can to stop me from having an abortion. If they have to, they will put me under a twenty-four-hour watch."

The wheels in my brain spun and spun until they screeched to a sudden stop.

They can't stop her if they can't find her.

—Lise

March 22
Early morning
Dear Ms. Tilson,

Lise has some wild idea about how I'm still going to have an abortion even after her mom tells my parents. At this point, I'm open to whatever idea she comes up with. I don't have many options, and I'm running out of time.

Daphne dropped me off down the street from my house, far enough away that they wouldn't see me get out of a strange car. It was well past 8 p.m., but I'd told Bethany I'd be staying for dinner at Susanna's, so I was covered. I trudged up toward my house, watching out for icy patches on the road. The cold was bone-deep. The calendar may say spring, but winter still has a tight hold here.

I was almost at my driveway, when I saw HIS car.

HE was here.

In my house.

Why? Why did he always have to come over? I couldn't breathe. Panic spread through me and rooted my feet to the ground. I needed to be safe. Away from him. Somewhere I could breathe. I wanted to be in my closet, hidden away in the dark. But to get there, I would have to walk through the front door and be polite and hospitable to the man who raped me.

I wanted to run.

I couldn't breathe.

And then I got angry. This was *my* house. I shouldn't have to run off because he was on *my* turf. And I thought, *What would Lise do?*

She would do what was best for *her*. Not for the family, certainly not for HIM. With her voice in my ear, I crept around to the back door. Inside, I took off my shoes and tiptoed upstairs. Then I shut myself in my closet. In that tight space, with my own familiar clothes hanging all around me, I could breathe again. I stayed there until I heard footsteps in the hall, and got out as Bethany was coming into the room.

She jumped when she saw me. "When'd you come in?"

"A little while ago."

"How was Susanna's?" She looked at me like she knew Susanna's had been a lie, and for the hundredth time I wondered if I told her, would she keep my secret or go running downstairs to tell Mom and Dad?

I couldn't risk it.

"Fine." My neck went red hot with shame and my stomach churned with nausea. I slid out of the room and went to the bathroom, trying to make it look casual and not desperate. I locked the door, put a towel against the crack between the door and the floor, and knelt in front of the toilet. But the sick never came. What was roiling in my stomach was not morning sickness, but rage.

I grabbed my towel and screamed into it. I screamed my shame, my fear, my anger that HE was chatting with my dad while I visited meth trailers and stripped in front of strangers. I screamed my rage at being reduced to using back doors—to the clinic, to my own home—and about anyone else having a say in what to do with my own body.

I screamed myself hoarse, but I didn't have any dreams last night for the first time since this nightmare began.

Signed,

Mellie Rivers

March 22
Later morning
Dear Ms. Tilson,

I woke up early this morning, before the sun. I slept soundly for the first time in weeks. And for the first time in weeks, there was hope inside me. Maybe Lise's plan would work. Maybe my parents would support me. Maybe everything would be okay.

Bethany was waking up when I headed downstairs. Joanie, who always got up before the rest of the house and had been trained to occupy herself without waking everyone else, was sitting on the living room floor, coloring in a fairy princess coloring book. I expected to find the kitchen empty, but Hannah was sitting on a stool at the island, a cup of steaming coffee in her hands.

"Morning," I said.

She blinked. "What? Oh, good morning."

I don't drink coffee very often, but Hannah had made a pot and the smell was too tempting to resist. I poured myself a cup, added a ton of cream and sugar, and sat across from her. Even though she was dressed, she hadn't put on any makeup yet, and her face was pale and drawn, dark circles under her eyes, which were usually bright and cheery. I examined her from across the table, taking her in in a way I hadn't done in a very long time. Maybe not since before she got engaged. She seemed different. Smaller. More contained. "What's going on?" I asked her.

"What do you mean?" she snapped.

I winced. She shook her head. "Sorry. I didn't mean to be snippy."

I leaned toward her. "Are you okay? You seem, I don't know, upset or something."

"I'm not upset. Why would I be upset? I just have a lot on my mind. That's all."

"Okay."

We sipped our coffee in silence. Her phone buzzed. She didn't even look at it. I did. The screen was filled with missed calls and texts from her fiancé. I couldn't read what they said from my angle, but I could see they were in all caps.

"Aren't you going to answer it?"

She shrugged. The phone buzzed again. She still didn't reach for it, but her fingers tightened on the mug, her knuckles turning white.

I could hear footsteps above us, running water in the pipes, and Joanie humming a cartoon theme song as she colored. Hannah didn't take notice. She seemed deep inside herself.

I watched her warily. I didn't know which Hannah was here today, Old Hannah or Almost Mrs. Talbot.

Years ago, Hannah used to talk to me. I was the next-oldest girl, so it was natural. But then she went to high school, fell into a clique with the other church girls her age, and got a boyfriend who became her fiancé. I got left by the wayside.

The phone buzzed again. Hannah ignored it. "Do you ever wonder what's on the other side?" she asked me instead.

That was a weird question. "Other side of what?"

"Of this." She waved her hand in the air. "All the stuff we're doing. I'm doing. You're doing. What do you even want to do with your life, Mellie?"

"I don't know."

"Yes, you do." Her voice was fierce and low. "You know, even if it's deep down."

She was staring at me so hard that I didn't dare lie. "Paint. I want to paint."

"Then do it. Don't let anyone—Dad, Mom, anyone—tell you not to."

Where was this coming from? It was the first time I'd ever heard Hannah talk like this. Well, maybe she had when we were kids and played imaginary games where we traveled to China in a hot-air balloon and raised pandas.

Hannah pushed back her chair, but I put my hand on her arm. "What do you want to do, Hannah?"

She looked away. "I'm doing it. Teaching, getting married. Having babies is what's on the other side of that."

"Is that what you want?" I kept my voice low. I didn't want Joanie to hear and tell Mom about this conversation in her innocent-but-tactless way.

It took a moment, but she faced me, her eyes on mine. "I want to travel," she said. "I want to teach English to kids in Asia, Eastern Europe, Africa."

The air between us was thick. That was impossible. Especially once she was married. Maybe they'd take one good trip, but then she would get pregnant, and there'd be no more traveling.

Footsteps pounded on the stairs. We turned away from each other as the rest of the family came down for breakfast. Later, when Bethany and I left for school, I saw Hannah in her fiancé's car when he picked her up to take her to work. His face was twisted and angry as he talked to her. She sunk down low in the seat.

I've seen my father talk to my mother like that.

I've seen Delia's father talk to her mother like that.

I've seen how ugly men can be when they feel like they're losing control. I've felt it. I'm carrying that anger's baby.

She should not marry someone who treats her like that. But if I tell her this, I will become the enemy, not him.

Signed,
Mellie Rivers

March 22

Dear Ms. Tilson—

I told Mom my idea, and she didn't say it was impossible. We talked it all out and came up with a plan. A good plan. I think. I hope.

I slipped a note into Mellie's locker this morning, telling her to meet me in the bathroom by the gym. This time there was no note telling me no. She was there when I got to the bathroom, leaning against the sink and drinking from her water bottle. "Hey."

"Hey."

She looked different, brighter almost, a sharper, clearer version of herself. "How are you doing?"

"Still pregnant," she said, and laughed this short, bitter laugh that wasn't joyful at all. Then she got quiet. "But, I'm ready to face whatever's on the other side of this."

"Are you?" I didn't mean to doubt her, but sometimes there

are things you just can't be ready for. But I wanted her to feel strong. "That's good, I guess."

"So what's your wild plan?"

"It's not wild," I said. I backed up against the bathroom door. "I talked to my mom and she thinks it will work."

"Okay, so what is it?"

"We go to Denver," I said. "You and me. We go to the sister clinic in Denver, and have it done there. My mom will call your parents, but they won't be able to find you before you have the abortion."

Mellie's brows pinched together. "We go to Denver. For two days. Where will we stay?"

"Oh, my mom has tons of friends we can stay with," I said, waving my hand at the insignificance of this problem. "She's making some calls."

"But…your mom won't be the one to do it." Her brows were still drawn tight, her eyes filled with worry.

"No. She won't." I hadn't really considered that. "Is that a problem?"

Mellie hunched her shoulders. "I trust her. I don't know the people at the clinic in Denver."

"They're good people. It's one of the few clinics left in the state. They're fighting the good fight, like my mom."

She gnawed at her lip. "I just really wanted your mom to be my doctor."

I reached out and grasped her hand. "I know. And if there

was some other way…I just don't see it. If my mom calls your parents while you're still in Wolverton, they'll get to you. It'll be much harder for them to find you in Denver." I tried to smile and squeezed her hand. "And I'll be there."

Mellie's brows smoothed a bit. "Thank God for that." She took a big, shaky breath. "Thank God for you. Have I told you that?"

"Eh." I waved my hand again. "When this is all over, you can buy me a big piece of red velvet cake."

Mellie snorted, but then her face drew sad again. "When this is all over," she whispered, "what is my life going to look like?"

I wanted to tell her that her life would be sunshine and roses and unicorns. But I could only tell the truth: "I don't know."

Sure, we might get her safely out of Wolverton to have the abortion, but what would happen when she came back? What would she be coming back to?

The landscape of that world hasn't been built yet.

—Lise

March 23
Dawn
Dear Ms. Tilson,

Three days from now, I won't be pregnant anymore. The nightmare will be over on Sunday.

A new nightmare can begin.

But I can't think about that yet. I have to get through this nightmare first before I can face the next one.

Today, instead of going home, I'm going to get into Lise's car, and we're going to drive through the mountains to Denver. We're going to stay with one of Alanna's friends, and then on Sunday, it'll be over. Probably around the same time my family will be in church.

Unless they're scouring the state to find me.

I don't know what they're going to do when they get the call from Alanna. I don't know what I'll be coming home to. But at least I won't be pregnant anymore.

And then maybe I can tell my parents the truth about what happened to me, along with Delia and everyone else. Maybe I'll be able to build something new with them, something based on honesty. I'm done lying. I just want truth from now on.

I don't want to lose my family. But I can't lose myself.

Signed,
Mellie Rivers

March 23

Dear Ms. Tilson—

My plan would've worked perfectly except for the fucking snow.

By the end of the school day, it was swirling down, but it wasn't a bad storm. I could still drive in it, still see several feet beyond my windshield. I was confident. I called my mom and told her we were leaving. "Drive safe," she said. "Be careful in the snow." I know how to drive in the snow; Mom taught me herself. I've lived here my whole life; I could drive the roads and hills of Wolverton blindfolded in the snow. I know how snow works, how it may look light and ethereal, but it is actually heavy and dangerous.

That's why I could tell we were in deep, deep shit before we even reached the pass.

The snow was starting to pile up by the time we reached the outskirts of town. The pass was still twenty miles away, and the storm was getting stronger, the snow coming down fast. Mellie peered out her window, her hand cupped against the glass. "This looks pretty bad," she said.

That was an understatement, but I didn't say that out loud. Instead, I said, "I've driven in snow worse than this. No big deal."

What I didn't say was that I've driven in bad snow, but not over the pass. In the mountains, when it snows like this, you build a fire and make some hot cocoa while you wait out the storm. But I'm sure Mellie knew that. She's lived here her whole life too. Though Mellie has never driven in snow. She doesn't have her license. She doesn't understand the concentration it takes to drive through a storm like this, whether you're in the mountains or not.

Beyond the reach of the streetlights in town, the snow looked even more menacing, swirling wildly with nothing to keep it in check. I clutched the steering wheel and leaned forward, squinting through the pathetic light my headlights gave off, even with the high beams. The snow snaked in the air in front of us, shifting back and forth in the ever-changing wind. The tires gripped and released, gripped and released, then we swerved. My hands clung to the wheel, fighting for control. I didn't dare take my eyes off the road.

Why didn't we leave school early? Why didn't we ditch last period?

By the time we made it to the pass, the gate was up. Even through the snow, it was easy to see the bright, reflective red sign barring the road. A state trooper's car was parked just beyond it.

"No," Mellie whispered. It was the most hopeless sound I'd ever heard.

I eased the SUV to a stop, the front fender inches from the gate, and we sat staring at the blockade as if we could make it go away. A moment later, a trooper got out of the car and came to my window. I rolled it down.

He looked at me, then at Mellie. "Pass is closed," he said, like I couldn't already see the big freaking gate and his car blocking my path.

"Is it really that bad?" I asked.

"It's pretty slick," the trooper said. "The storm is supposed to get worse overnight." He squinted at us. "Where you girls headed in this kind of weather?"

"Denver."

He shook his head. "You'll have to wait for your girls' weekend."

I grit my jaw. "We're not having a 'girls' weekend.' She has a medical appointment."

"On a Friday night?" His blue eyes flashed his doubt. "Your parents know where you are?"

"Of course they do," I said through my teeth. "Thank you, Officer." I rolled up the window before he could say anything else, threw the car in reverse, and did a slippery three-point turn. Then I pulled to the side of the road and hit the call button on the Bluetooth System. It rang once before Mom answered with a breathless "Hello?"

"They've closed the pass. We have to turn around. Don't call them yet."

There was a split second of silence that passed in slow motion. I knew what she was going to say, and I wanted to live in that split second before she said it.

"I already made the call."

Next to me, Mellie made an inhuman sound, like an animal caught in a trap. Wolverton has trapped us. Within its boundaries, nowhere is safe until the storm passes.

—Lise

March 23
Dear Ms. Tilson,

Fear is a strange thing. It's not invisible. It has teeth so sharp you can feel them in your skin. It will eat you alive, and you can't do anything to stop it.

That's how I feel as Lise drives us back into Wolverton. Like I'm being eaten alive by fear.

I want to cry, but I've lost the strength.

"It'll be okay," Lise says, over and over. I want to believe her. But she's wrong. The fear is wrapped so tight around me, I don't know how I'm still alive. Shouldn't the fear just kill me? Isn't "scared to death" a phrase for a reason?

But I haven't died. Somehow, I'm still alive.

Lise keeps driving.

Lise keeps telling me, "It'll be okay."

My heart keeps beating.

My family knows. And they are close. I can feel them.

Deep down, I know the reckoning will come, but as long as I'm in this car, I don't have to face it. I can just live in this moment for as long as Lise's gas tank holds out.

I look over at Lise, hunched over the steering wheel, her eyes fixed on the snow-covered road in front of her.

I hold my hand out. Without a word, she takes hers off the steering wheel and squeezes my fingers.

"It'll be okay," she says again.

I still don't believe her…but I believe that she believes it, and that has to be enough.

Signed,
Mellie Rivers

March 23
(Again)
Dear Ms. Tilson—

When I was seven, my dad hit a deer with our Toyota Highlander. Ten years later, I can still hear the screech of the tires, feel the thud of the deer's body as our car crashed into it. And I can still see its eyes. You know that saying, "a deer in the headlights"? When you see a real deer in real headlights, you truly understand that saying.

That's all I could think about when I looked over at Mellie in the passenger seat. She had that same look in her eyes. Like she was about to meet her doom.

The thing is, I couldn't guarantee that she wasn't.

I headed back to town, because there was nowhere else to go. There's only one road in and out of Wolverton and all the roads in between lead to Mellie's parents.

Mellie leaned back in her seat and covered her face with her hands. I couldn't tell if she was crying or not. Her whole body was shaking, but she didn't make a sound.

"It'll be okay," I said. They felt like the emptiest words I'd ever spoken.

"How?" Mellie pulled her hands away from her face. She wasn't crying. Her expression was so terrified it was beyond crying. "Where am I gonna go?"

"We'll find someplace safe. My house."

"Lise, they probably already know about your mom now. We can't put her in more danger."

Shit, she's right. I kept driving, my mind a blank. We rolled back into town. Streetlights pooled on the ground, giving the snow a soft glow, making it look kinder and gentler than it actually was. No one was out on the roads. Why would they be? Everyone's hunkered down, ready to wait out the storm.

I slowed down at the stop sign at the base of Ridge Road. That's Mellie's neighborhood. Her nails dug into the seat as headlights swept down the hill. A silver SUV slowly descended in the snow.

"It's my father," Mellie breathed.

I stepped on the gas, even though I hadn't come to a complete stop. "Get down," I told her, and Mellie ducked under the shoulder strap of her seat belt and crouched on the floor so she wouldn't be visible as we blasted through the intersection. A block later, I glanced in my rearview mirror.

They were following us.

"Shit."

"Oh God. They're following us, aren't they?" Mellie said.

"I can lose them."

I took a hard right before we hit the high school. Mellie's dad followed. Who the hell did he think I was? Why did he think his daughter was in this particular car? All I could imagine was that following me gave him some sense of purpose, that he could at least feel as if he was trying to find her.

We climbed the hill into the Snowy Pines development where Cara lives. For an instant, I considered going to her house, but there was no way I could lose Mellie's dad before we got there. I turned left, then right, then right again until I was at the top of the development, winding along the road that encircles it. The whole way, Mellie's father followed, not too close, but close enough that he could see every turn I made. I'd have to figure out a way to leave Snowy Pines without looking suspicious, because why would someone drive up here if not to go somewhere specific? It's not exactly good weather.

Then I remembered: Cara and her family were away. They went to Colorado Springs for the weekend. She skipped school today so they could beat the weekend traffic...and the storm.

I flicked on my blinker to take the next right. The silver SUV did the same. Cara's house was on the next block and, thank goodness, her car was in the driveway, making it look like someone was home. I pulled into the driveway and turned off the car.

"Stay down," I told Mellie and tossed her a blanket from the back seat. She pulled it over herself so she was a fluffy, purple lump.

I hopped out and walked up to Cara's front door, head bent against the swirling snow. There was a light on in the front room. Cara's mom leaves it on whenever they go away so the house doesn't look empty. At that moment, I loved Cara's mom. When I got to the porch, I turned to see Mellie's father drive by slowly—so freaking slowly it was like the world had gone into slow motion. Someone in the passenger seat of the SUV rolled down the window and stuck her head out to watch me. It was Mellie's mom.

I knocked on the door, my heart pounding against my ribs. After a moment, I looked back. The street was empty. Down at the corner, the SUV turned onto the road that leads out of the development. I waited until its taillights disappeared, then raced back to my car. As I threw it into reverse, Mellie's head popped up.

"Are they gone?" she whispered.

"For now."

I took us the back way out of Snowy Pines, putting us at the high school. I peered up and down Main Street, looking for the silver SUV. It was nowhere to be seen.

But I couldn't breathe. This was hour one. We still have forty-seven more to get through.

—Lise

March 23
(Still)
Dear Ms. Tilson—

I took Mellie to Rowan's house, because I couldn't think of anywhere else to go.

The snow piled up, the side of the road lined by deep drifts that encased the trees so the brown of their trunks disappeared into the white. By the time we pulled into Rowan's driveway, I knew we were going to have to stay put.

The lights inside his house glowed golden soft through the windows. I was so happy to be there that, for a second, I didn't feel afraid. Anywhere with Rowan was safety. Sanctuary.

When we got out of the car, Mellie tilted her head to the sky. Snow dusted her eyelashes and turned her eyebrows white. "We're stuck here, aren't we?"

"I think so."

We hung on to each other as we made our way up the slippery

walk. At the front porch, I turned back and scanned the road. No cars. Rowan doesn't live on a main street, but if Mr. Rivers made his way over here, he would surely recognize my car from Snowy Pines.

Rowan and his mom can lock the doors, bar the windows, even call the police, but how long can we keep Mellie safe? We can't legally keep the mayor from his own daughter. There are still forty-six hours left in the waiting period, and we still have to get Mellie to the clinic. Anything can happen between now and then, between here and there. Time is not on our side.

I knocked on the door.

After a minute, Rowan opened it. "Hey!" His face widened into a smile. "I thought you were going away this weekend!" His gaze slid from me to Mellie, and back to me. "What's going on?"

"Can we come in?"

"Yeah, sure. Of course."

Rowan's house always smells like something delicious just came out of the oven. Half the time it has. We followed him into the kitchen, where Rosemary was pulling out a tray of muffins. They smelled amazing. "Lise, honey! And Mellie! What a nice surprise."

"Hi, Rosemary."

"What brings you over in this weather? I was sure everyone was hunkered down. I closed the gallery early. The roads are terrible."

I peered out their big bay window that takes up half the wall in the living room. Rowan's house is all open space and glass, which should feel cold, but somehow Rosemary makes it the opposite. I didn't know what to say to her. It wasn't my place to tell her what was really going on. The rumble of a car engine echoed outside. Mellie dashed around the back of the island counter, ready to duck out of sight. I held my breath. The car engine grew closer, closer, closer…a pickup truck crawled past. I recognized it as Jason Bellows's, who lives one street over from Rowan. When the truck disappeared from view, I leaned over the counter where Mellie was crouched. "It wasn't him," I said. She straightened.

"Okay," Rowan said, "what the hell is going on?"

"Rowan."

I'd never heard Rosemary sound so sharp. She's always hippie-soft. She had this knowing look on her face, but she couldn't possibly know. Could she? Rosemary does have an abundance of woman's intuition, and it was clearly kicking in. "Why don't you girls go into the TV room? Rowan and I will be right in with some tea and muffins."

The TV room is behind the kitchen, safely away from the street. She calls it the TV room because it's the only room in the house that has one. I love their big flat-screen television, and the squishy leather couch and chairs with all their pillows and ridiculously warm-and-cozy faux-fur throw blankets. It's aggressively comfortable. Rowan and I have spent many hours curled up watching movies or Netflix marathons, and those blankets are also great because they hide hands that might be in compromising places if a parent were to walk in unannounced.

After settling on the couch, I pulled out my phone. "We need to call my mom. She's probably freaking out." I dialed the number and put it on speaker.

Mom answered on the first ring. "Where are you?"

"Rowan's house."

There was an audible sigh. "Okay, good. That seems safe for now."

"For now?" Mellie asked, her voice trembling.

Mom heard it too. "Mellie, honey, how are you holding up?"

I watched Mellie's face as she tried to answer. Her pupils looked enormous beneath a shiny surface of tears. "Not good," she finally whispered.

"Mr. Rivers followed us through town," I said. "He didn't know Mellie was in the car, but still. It was—"

"Terrifying," Mellie finished for me. I wondered what that had been like for her, hiding under a blanket while her dad followed us. Terrifying seemed too small a word for that.

"Jesus." Mom's anger and helplessness was palpable through the phone. "Okay, look. You'll have to spend the night at Rowan's. Hopefully as it gets darker and the snow gets worse, he'll give up the search."

"But we still have to get her to the clinic."

"I know."

"Can't we just do it tomorrow?" I asked.

"Lise, you know the law. The waiting period is forty-eight hours. If we can get through tomorrow..."

She trailed off and I knew we were all thinking the same thing. Tomorrow seemed endless.

"What are you going to tell Rosemary?" Mom asked.

"I don't know," I said, looking at Mellie. There were shadows on her face that hadn't been there before.

"The truth," Mellie said, "I want to tell her the truth."

"I can talk to her if you want," Mom offered.

"No," Mellie said. "I'll tell her myself."

"Okay," Mom said. Static crackled on the line. "Lise, honey, you have my permission to tell her about my job. She has an I STAND WITH PLANNED PARENTHOOD sticker as her Facebook profile picture, so I think we can trust her."

I'd noticed that too; she'd had it up ever since the shooting at that clinic last year. It would be a relief to tell Rosemary. "Can I tell Rowan too?"

"Yes, honey, you can."

I exhaled a shaky breath. I just hoped he wouldn't be mad at me for not telling him the truth sooner.

"Okay, call me later. Love you."

"I love you too, Mom."

The phone clicked off. Mellie and I looked at each other. I wondered what she saw in my face. What I saw in her face was that she was on the verge of tears. I settled her into one of the oversized chairs and tucked a faux-fur blanket around her. Rosemary came in carrying a tray with a teapot, three mugs, and a plate of muffins. She set it down on the coffee table. I looked past her. "Where's Rowan?" I asked.

"I told him to give us some time," Rosemary said. "I thought maybe this should be a girls-only conversation."

Do you see what I mean about intuition? She has it. Then another thought occurred to me. "Hey, where's Saul?" That's Rowan's dad. He's not around a ton because of his work, but when he is, he likes to be involved in everything.

"In Los Angeles for business." She gave an overdramatic sigh. "It's eighty-five degrees there today. He's probably surfing. Bastard."

I forced a laugh. I like Saul, but maybe it was better he wasn't here. It was one less person that Mellie would have to talk to.

Rosemary poured us tea. "It's rooibos, no caffeine," and handed us each a muffin, "blueberry bran, good for the digestion." Then she pulled over one of the floor pillows and sat down with her legs crossed.

"Look," she began, "I'm not going to make you tell me anything you don't want to. But you came to my house—which is fine, my door is always open—and you're hiding from cars driving down the street, and you both look scared, so obviously something is up. By being here, you've involved me, so I think I need some context."

This is what is so great about Rosemary. A lot of other parents would just say, "I'm the adult, you're the child, spill." She treats you like an equal…while letting you know, in no uncertain terms, you'd better tell her the truth.

I looked over at Mellie.

After a long sip of tea, Mellie set down her mug.

And started to talk.

—Lise

Somehow, it is still March 23,
the longest day of my life
Dear Ms. Tilson,

I've never had a boyfriend, so I don't know what it's like to show up at his house unannounced. At Rowan's house, we're greeted with warm smiles, tea, and homemade muffins. Is this what happens everywhere? Is that how normal people behave?

Rowan's house is nothing like mine. It's more modern, with sharper angles and more open space and glass. And from the moment Lise and I walked in, I could tell the people who live here are happy. They don't retreat to their separate corners, coveting their privacy in a house that has none. They respect each other. They like each other.

That's why when Lise's mom asked us what we're going to tell Rosemary, I said, "The truth."

When I first met Rosemary at the art gallery last week, she touched my arm while she talked, looked me in the eyes, and listened to what I had to say. I didn't give it a lot of thought at the time, because I was so nervous about going to the clinic afterward, but I remembered it now.

This house is just like her. Warm. Inviting. Comforting. Sanctuary. That gripping, paralyzing fear I felt in Lise's car as we wound through Snowy Pines with Dad right behind us was ebbing away. I know he's still out there looking for me, but in Rosemary's house, I feel safe.

So when she asked us to tell her what's going on and Lise looked at me to lead the way, I told the truth. No more lies.

And it feels good. It almost feels better than when I told Lise.

While I talked, Rosemary reached out and touched my knee. Occasionally interjected with an "Oh, honey."

Lise filled in her side of the story, about her mom and the clinic. Rosemary shook her head, her eyes sad. "I hate that you felt like you had to carry that all by yourself, Lise."

After we finished, Rosemary gave me a long, hard hug, and I could tell she wanted to cry—for me, for every girl who's ever been in my shoes. When she pulled back, she brushed a lock of hair away from my face. My heart hurt when she did that. It should've been my own mother doing that, not someone else's. My own mother should be the one protecting me.

"I had one," Rosemary said, so quiet I almost didn't hear her. Startled, I looked up into her face. She had this faraway look in her eyes, like she was peering into the edge of her memory. "It was when I was in college. I dated this guy for a few months. The condom broke. We had already split up by the time I found out I was pregnant. There wasn't a question that I wouldn't keep it."

I stilled. It wasn't the same as when Alanna told me she'd been raped too. Rosemary had sex by choice, and then made the decision she needed when she discovered she was pregnant. She wasn't like the women the PCC insinuated I would become if I had one. She's a mother. A successful business owner. An artist.

Without taking a breath, I asked her the one question that has haunted me.

"Do you regret it?"

She tilted her head to the side. "No. I don't regret it. Am I sad that I was in that situation? Yes. But it wasn't my fault. It wasn't anybody's fault—"

"Except the condom company's," Lise muttered.

Rosemary snorted. "Well, they never claim to be one hundred percent effective. I still took the risk, because I wanted to have sex, and I don't regret that. But I was twenty years old. I wasn't ready to be a mother. And I had no support system. If I'd had that child, I wouldn't have finished school or gone on to grad school...and that's where I met Rowan's dad. So I wouldn't have met him, married him, had Rowan, moved here, and opened the gallery. Or been an artist. I would've been too busy struggling to make ends meet."

Hearing that Rosemary didn't regret her decision made me jittery, like I'd just discovered something wonderful and rare. If she could stand by herself and her decision, maybe I could too.

"I know some people will say things happen for a reason or are fated," Rosemary went on, "but I think we all have a choice. This is your life. You have a say in how you want to live it. If you don't want to be a mother at sixteen, then you shouldn't have to be."

I don't know why, but it's this that makes me feel like I can let go of my guilt and someday have a life like hers. Rosemary's story gives me hope that I can be a mother in my own time, on my own terms.

"Thank you," I told her, but those seem like such small words in comparison to the enormous gift she had given me.

After that, Lise went upstairs to talk to Rowan, and Rosemary went off to get sheets for the pullout couch and our overnight bags from the car. And that's where I am now, lying in the pulled-out bed, writing all this down in my journal. Seeing it on paper helps me make some sense of it.

Lise just came back.

When she saw me writing in my journal, she laughed and pulled hers from her backpack. Her notebook looks a lot fuller than mine. She must've started it earlier than I did. She changed into her sweats and climbed into the bed next to me.

We're writing in silence together, the only sound that of our pens scratching against the paper.

Signed,
Mellie Rivers

Edited to Add: When Lise stopped writing, we both looked at each other. And without a word, we exchanged journals and began reading.

March 23 (because yes, there is still more to write about today)

Dear Ms. Tilson—

Rowan wasn't mad. He didn't ask me to tell him everything. He only wanted to know that I was okay.

I told him I was, but that Mellie was in trouble. And I had to help her.

"Of course you did. That's what you do. Help people."

He's said this before, and Cara has said it—hell, everyone who knows me has said it—but this time it really sank in. It's true. Helping people is what I do. It was like a gear that's always been loose inside me clicked into place. That is what I want to do with my life. This is *my* thing, like Rowan has writing and Mellie has art and Cara has fashion. I want to go into politics. I want to effect change that helps people. I want to make laws that will make people's lives better. I want to create a world where girls don't have to go through what Mellie is going through.

When I realized this, I burst into tears.

I cried for a long time, until my eyes hurt.

Rowan was a little beside himself, but he sat with me and let me cry.

I don't even know why I was crying. Maybe it's relief at finally knowing what I'm meant to do. Maybe it's sorrow and fear for Mellie. But maybe it's something deeper and more complicated. I thought about what Mellie would be doing if I hadn't followed her into the bathroom after gym class. Would she have taken the PCC's advice and decided to keep the baby? Would she have gone through with the abortion in that trailer? Would she have made her own decision, or would someone have made it for her?

I don't know the answers to any of these questions.

I believe what Rosemary told Mellie, that we should be free to make our own choices, to determine our own fate.

I also believe that sometimes fate gives us a little push, and we should let ourselves be pushed. That's why I followed Mellie that first day. Was it fate? For all Mellie has gone through, it brought us together. I can't imagine life without her now. She helped me to realize my purpose in life.

After I cried myself out, Rowan and I talked for a long time. I told him about my mom, and what she does, and why I had to hide it from him. I think he was a little hurt that I didn't trust him with that secret. And that I told Mellie about it before my dedicated, loyal, longtime boyfriend. But he said he understood. I think he does.

Now Mellie and I are on the pullout bed in the TV room, writing in our journals. I want her to read what I've written. I feel like she has a right to that. She's been the main topic of this journal for the last few weeks. She should read it. It's only fair.

I don't know what's going to happen tomorrow. We still have another thirty-eight hours to get through. Maybe Mr. Rivers won't find us here. Maybe tomorrow will pass uneventfully, and we'll get her to the clinic unseen, and everything will be fine.

But somehow I think that fate isn't quite done with us yet.

—Lise

March 24
Dear Ms. Tilson,

Lise's phone woke me up.

I can't believe I actually slept, but I did, and really well. Next to me, Lise moaned and grabbed her phone from the table next to her. She checked the text and sat up. "Mom's on her way over."

When I walked into the kitchen, the light from the windows was blinding. It's a wonderland outside, the landscape white and crystalline, like a postcard you'd find at an Aspen resort. The snow was piled up to the windowsills, the roads pristine and unplowed. "How the heck is your mom going to get here?" I asked Lise.

"On skis."

And sure enough, several minutes later, she came into view, striding down the street on cross-country skis. Wow. I've seen other people do that when it snows, but *my* mom would never be one of them.

I want to be the kind of woman who skis through town after a blizzard.

Alanna brought in a blast of cold with her when she opened the door. "We're definitely stuck here for a while." She wrapped her hands around a mug of coffee that Rosemary poured for her. "The plows are still out on the main road through the passes. I doubt they'll get to town until later today at the earliest."

Lise looked between us. "So what do we do? Hunker down here and hope Mr. Rivers doesn't find us?"

"Why would he?" Alanna asked. "I think we're safe. I'm just worried about getting to the clinic tomorrow."

I think we're safe. I've latched on to those words. Lise's car is buried under snow out front, but if my dad recognizes it... He saw Lise yesterday, and he knows that she and I are friends... There are many dots to connect, but whether he'd be able to put them together in time, I don't know.

Rosemary made us all pancakes and we ate around her big dining room table made out of reclaimed barn wood. It's all so normal and nice, like she does this every Saturday morning. Which she probably does. She makes pancakes for her son and her friends who ski over to her house through the snow. Saturday mornings at my house revolve around whatever campaign stop Dad has to make that day.

Most of the day has passed like that. Quiet. Cozy. Curled up safe from the cold outside. Me, Lise, and Rowan settled in for a

Parks and Rec marathon while Rosemary and Alanna hung out in the kitchen. We could hear their laughter from the TV room. As if there is nowhere they would rather be on a day like today.

I'm writing this all down because I need to document it. I need to have written proof that what I'm doing isn't going to end the world, that I can make this decision and there can be still be good things in life like pancakes and lazy Saturdays spent with Netflix. That people will still love me when it's

HE'S HERE.

I HAVE TO GO.

March 24
Ms. Tilson—

He found us.

I can't think. I need to think. Which is why I'm writing right now. It's helping me think. Where did she go? Where would Mellie go?

My mom—no, I can't think about her now. I need to figure out where Mellie is.

She ran out the back door when she heard his voice booming through Rosemary and Rowan's house like he owned it. His knocking on the door reverberated in my bones. That's how loud it was. It felt like the house was going to collapse on our heads. I think maybe my house did collapse on my head today.

Before Rosemary even opened the door, Mellie knew it was him. I could see it in her eyes, that deer-in-headlights look.

I was on my feet in an instant and into the kitchen, Rowan right behind me. Rosemary opened the door. Without being asked, without even saying, "Hello, I'm Mr. Rivers, do you know where my daughter is?" he barged in, pushing past Rosemary to march up to me.

"Where's my daughter?"

"Excuse me!" Rosemary bellowed, her Mama Bear coming out. "Who the hell do you think you are?"

Mr. Rivers ignored her. "Where is my daughter?" he repeated, advancing on me. Before he could get to me, Mom stepped in, putting herself between us.

"Back away from my daughter, Mr. Rivers," she said. She was so strong, so calm, like a mountain facing off with a tsunami.

Mr. Rivers flicked his gaze from me to her. "You," he growls. "You're the doctor who called me."

The room fell silent.

Mr. Rivers knows. He knows about my mom.

Mellie is gone, and Mayor Rivers knows about my mom. Everything I've done to protect both of them has failed.

I feel empty. This must be what it feels like to have lost all hope.

If Mr. Rivers knows about Mom, what is he going to do with that information? I can't—Mom had to be scared, but she did not show it. She was just focused on Mellie. That's what I have to focus on now—

One thing at a time, Lise, one thing at time.

I have to figure out where Mellie is before I can do anything else.

Mr. Rivers stormed out once he realized Mellie was not in the house. He is looking for her. He's looking for her right now. He has a head start, he'll find her before I do...

I have no idea where she went.

Think, Lise. *Think.*

Tracks lead out the back door and disappear on the road behind Rowan's house, which got plowed a couple of hours ago. *Where would she go?*

School is closed. She can't go home. She wouldn't go to another friend's house, because I'm the only one who knows what is happening.

I wish I were religious. This is when I'd start praying. But I do have faith—in myself—

Wait.

I KNOW WHERE SHE IS.

March 24
(I have lost track of time)
Dear Ms. Tilson,

When everything else is closed, God is always open.

I was out the back door of Rosemary's house before I knew where I was going, but somehow my feet brought me here. Somehow I knew the church would be open, even if half the roads are still unplowed and the pile of snow against the front doors is so high that I had to go in through the side door.

I think someone might be here, in the back offices. There's a light on and every once in a while I hear a cough. Whoever it is didn't hear me come in. I snuck up through the balcony to the little alcove behind the organ. Tucked in there, it's quiet and warm. It feels safe here. The only other person who knows about it is the organist.

Well, there is one more person.

Years ago, when Lise and I were in Girl Scouts together, we

were paired for an exercise. The troop was still new and it was one of those getting-to-know-you games, where you tell the other person one thing about yourself, and she tells you one thing, and then you switch partners and learn something new about everybody until you're all best friends by the end of the meeting.

Lise went first. She said that the week before she'd been horseback riding for the first time, and she loved it so much that all she wanted to do was ride horses, morning, noon, and night, that she wanted to ride horses for the rest of her life. She was afraid to tell her parents because she knew how expensive and all-consuming it was to have a horse and they'd never buy one for her.

I remember being impressed that Lise understood words like "expensive" and "all-consuming." We were only six, and I was just starting to learn that Mommy and Daddy couldn't give me everything I asked for. Especially since there was another kid on the way, and who knew how many after that? (One more, as it turned out. But it was enough.) And I remember being really jealous that Lise was an only child. What was that like to have all your parents' attention?

She looked at me, expectant, ready to hear what I was going to share.

There were so many things I could've said.

I feel like my parents have so many kids and not a big enough capacity to love for all of them.

I feel like I'm not as special as my sister, because she was born first, or my brother, because he is a boy.

I feel like I'm not supposed to dream big, that I should dream very, very small, because that's all I'm going to get.

But I didn't tell her any of those things. Instead, I told her about this place. It's so quiet, I told her, not like my own house, which is always filled with noise. After church, when my parents were talking with the other adults at coffee hour and my older brother and sister were off playing with their friends, I would come here, to be in the quiet.

To hear my own thoughts.

To hear my heart.

To hear God.

In this quiet, I can hear myself now.

My own thoughts. Not anyone else's.

I've done so much thinking since that pink line appeared on the stick. I've thought myself to exhaustion. When I heard Dad's voice booming through Rosemary's house, I stopped thinking. I ran. I ran until I knew they couldn't find me, and now I'm hiding again. I've spent as much time hiding as thinking.

As I write this, I realize I'm done with both.

I'm done thinking. I've made my choice, and I'm ready to act on it. In order to do that, I can't hide anymore.

When I was hiding under that blanket in Lise's car… I don't

ever want to feel like that again. I don't want to be weak. I don't want anyone else to save me. I want to save myself.

It's time to step into the open. My parents can't chase me around this town forever. I have to tell them the truth. They have as much right to hear it as I have to say it. Even if they don't believe me, I know the truth. No one can take that away from me.

There are footsteps coming up the stairs.

Pastor Charlie?

No, too light to be him.

Who…

Of course.

Even after all these years, she remembered. "We don't have to go down," she said. "We can stay here."

"No," I told her. "It's time to stop hiding."

Signed,

Mellie Rivers

March 24
Dear Ms. Tilson,

At the beginning of this journal I wrote how I had everything but didn't know it.

What I meant was, I had nothing, because it was built on lies.

Now, I have nothing.

But that nothing is built on truth.

So I have everything.

Signed,
Mellie Rivers

March 24
(Still)
This day will go on in me for a long time
Dear Ms. Tilson,

I'm a few hours removed from what happened, and I think I can write about it now. The scene is still replaying in my mind like a movie on repeat. Maybe if I write it all out, I can move on. Maybe that's what you had in mind all along when you handed us these journals, that by writing down all our innermost thoughts we can let it all go and get on with our lives.

Lise and I climbed down from the church balcony. Outside, the sunlight hurt my eyes. In the car, she called her mom to tell her where we were going.

I told her not to.

It was too dangerous for her, I said. "He has guns in the house."

Lise glanced at me. "If I go in there without backup, my mother will kill me herself."

So we called for backup: Alanna, Rosemary, and Rowan.

We all got to the house at the same time. Lise gripped my arm as we walked up the driveway. "Are you ready?"

No. But I was never going to be ready. I don't think you're ever ready for moments like this.

The front door opened before we reached it. Dad stepped outside and pointed at Alanna. "That woman"—he spat—"is not welcome in my house."

"I'm not going inside without her," I said. "So you can let her in or we can have this out on the front lawn where all the neighbors can see."

"What kind of lies have you been telling my daughter?" he snarled at Alanna.

"None!" I yelled back before Alanna could answer. "She's helping me…more than you or Mom have. You have it all wrong about that clinic, Dad."

Mom appeared in the doorway like Dad's shadow. "Please, please come inside," she said quietly, looking at the surrounding houses. I followed her gaze across the street. A front curtain twitched, as though someone had been watching. Dad must've seen too, because he stepped aside.

I didn't know what to expect inside. I half expected to see Jeremy guarding the Rivers family turf with a shotgun. Instead, he was sitting on the stairs. Hannah stood in the entry to the kitchen, her face pale. Bethany and my younger sisters were nowhere to be seen. I think if they'd been there, I would've faltered.

It hurts so much right now, thinking about how I've broken my family. Or did my family break me? I don't know. The pain threads through everything, like a circle with no beginning or ending. Is there ever going to be a day when it stops hurting so much?

Dad closed the door behind us once we were all inside. Lise had joked that our door is like a dungeon door, and for the first time in my life, I got that. It felt like we were being locked in.

Dad and Mom came around to face me, Hannah and Jeremy behind them. My own army fanned out around me. Okay, I thought. If this is a battle, then here we go.

I fired the first shot. "I was raped," I said before anyone else could talk.

I wish I could write that my mom collapsed crying, or my dad grabbed me into a big bear hug, and that Jeremy swore he'd kill the guy who did it. I wish I could say there were tears and promises of support, and that no matter what decision I made about the pregnancy, they'd be there for me. I wish I had that family. You've read enough of this journal by now to know I don't have that family.

My brain has blocked some of what happened right after I said those words. What I remember comes in slices, like photographs torn in half.

Slice. Mom's mouth moving without sound.

Slice. Jeremy's folded arms, his face pinched with doubt.

Slice. Dad saying, "You have to take responsibility" in a clear, firm tone.

What I remember most was my army coming to life. "You think she's lying?" Lise yelled.

"I think you're refusing to take responsibility for your actions," Dad said to me, not even acknowledging Lise.

"I was not responsible for the action that made me pregnant," I said.

"Even if that were true," Jeremy said, "it's a baby, Mellie. It's a life. Don't punish the baby."

I wanted to punch him. "You have no idea what you're talking about, Jeremy. The only one being punished here is me."

"You have no right to take an innocent life—"

"My life is worth something too—"

"Who was it?"

Hannah spoke for the first time since I entered the house. She stepped away from the frame of the kitchen doorway.

I looked her in the eye.

Everyone else in the room disappeared.

It felt like just me and her, alone in the world.

I made my lips say his name.

"Brandon."

Brandon Talbot.

Pastor Charlie's son.

Delia's brother.

Hannah's fiancé.

Now you know, Ms. Tilson.

"He raped me downstairs in the basement. Right before Christmas."

"That's a goddamned lie," Jeremy said.

"I would've noticed," Mom said. "Your behavior afterward would've—"

"All you noticed was the laundry got done," I said, my eyes still on Hannah. She believed me. I could tell from her face. She believed me because she knew he had that in him.

Mom collapsed into the nearest chair. Her lips were white and her cheeks splotchy. I want to know what she was thinking. Did she believe me? Did she think back over the last several weeks and realize how absent she's been from my life?

"You didn't report it," Dad said. His voice, his posture, his eyes—they all accused me. "If it happened, why didn't you report it?"

"I didn't want to hurt Hannah," I said softly. She hadn't moved. "I thought I could forget it happened. But then…" I splayed my hand out over my stomach.

"Oh God," Hannah gasped and fled into the kitchen. She made it to the sink before she vomited. For several minutes the only sound was her retching. I wanted to go to her, but Dad was blocking my way, and I had to hold my ground.

Dad stared at me. "I'm having a hard time believing you, Mellie." It was his I'm-disappointed-in-you voice, the one I used to be afraid of, but now pissed me off. I folded my arms. "If it happened like you said, you would've reported it."

"Sixty-three percent of rapes go unreported," Alanna cut in. "It's the most underreported crime. Probably because people in positions of authority don't believe the victim. Or they blame the victim."

"Nobody asked you," Dad growled at her.

"Hey!" I stepped close to him so we were inches apart. "Don't talk to her like that. She's been helping me, far more than my own family."

Dad brought his face close to mine. "You know what I think? I think you've been jealous of Hannah ever since she got engaged, and you seduced Brandon to get one over on her. I know how women work," he said. "And now you're carrying the consequence of your actions, and you want to take the easy way out." I could feel his breath on my nose. "I thought I raised you better."

I want to say that his words sent a shiver down my spine. Or that he made me cry. But all I felt was contempt. I looked deep in his eyes. "And I thought I had a father. But all I have is a mayor."

He jerked back.

I stepped around him and broke the circle. "I'm having this abortion," I said. "I won't give birth to my rapist's baby. I won't do it."

"Every baby is a blessing," Mom said. "Even those that come to us in the worst circumstances."

"No, Mom," I said, "not every baby is a blessing."

"She's gotten to you." Dad pointed at Alanna. "These people are insidious, Mellie. After all we've done for you, you choose to listen to her instead of your own family?"

"No, I'm choosing to listen to myself." My voice was steady. "She never once told me to have an abortion. All she told me was that the choice was mine. It's my body, and I get to choose."

"No, it's not," Dad shot back. "This is God's choice. However it happened, He chose to give you a baby—"

"'However it happened'? Brandon forced himself on me!" I was so angry I could feel it lighting up my skin. "I didn't choose that. But I get to choose what happens now. And I won't spend my life raising this baby."

"Give it up for adoption," Jeremy said.

"I can raise it," Mom said in a small voice. I heard it there inside those words, that desperation for another baby. The six she already had were never enough.

"No," Dad said. "Hannah can raise the baby."

In the movies, during a dramatic moment, sometimes everyone turns to stare at one person. I swear it happened like that. A shudder went through me. I think deep inside, I knew this would be their solution, and that the abortion wasn't just for me. It was to save Hannah too.

"He will be her husband in a few weeks," Dad continued while everyone else stared at him. "We'll send Mellie away to have the baby. The child will be Hannah's niece or nephew. It might as well be her own."

I'm still asking myself: Did he really say that? It's like a plot-line right out of a bad made-for-television movie. None of this should ever happen to anyone in real life.

And it won't. Not to me.

Hannah walked back from the sink, wiping her mouth on a dish towel. "No," she said, and she threw the dish towel at him. "No," she repeated.

"No, what?" Dad challenged. Mom was still in the chair, her arms wrapped around herself. Jeremy looked like he was going to hit Hannah. But she stared straight at my dad and put her hands on her hips. Like freaking Wonder Woman.

"No, I will not raise Mellie's baby," she said. "And no, I will not be getting married to that man. Because yes," she crossed in front of Dad and stood next to me, "I believe her. And I will support whatever Mellie chooses to do." She snaked her arm around my waist and pulled me to her side. Big sister, little sister.

I had to stop writing to lay my head down and sob. Right now, Hannah is sitting in Rosemary's kitchen, being taken care of with tea and comfort food. After we left our house, we came back here and she collapsed on the couch, as if all the fight went out of her in one whoosh. She cried for hours. Hannah stood up for me even though I destroyed her life. And even though she insists that she's relieved she's not getting married, I know her heart is broken too.

I didn't really think about how Hannah was going to react to the truth. I think I never let myself imagine it, because I was so scared of losing her along with everyone else. I never imagined she'd take my side. I guess I thought she'd take Brandon's.

You can never assume anything about anyone. You think you know someone, but people are unpredictable. There's danger in that, but there is also beauty. And for all the ugly that happened today, her standing up for me was beautiful, and I will love Hannah forever for that.

After she took my side, Dad just stared at us like we were strangers. He was already writing us off. "If you go through with this, you are no longer part of this family," he said. "Both of you. You are not welcome in this house, and you are not to associate with any member of my family."

"Hiram." Mom's voice broke on his name. Tears streaked her face.

"What?" Dad snapped at her. She didn't say anything else, just buried her face in her hands.

I opened my mouth, but Hannah's fingers tightened on my waist and I shut it. I trusted her to talk for me. "Dad," she said.

"Yes?"

Ms. Tilson, I swear there was a note of hope in his voice. But what did he think we were going to say? Did he actually think we would agree to his plan?

"I won't be voting for you in the upcoming elections," Hannah said. Then she turned us around and marched us out the front door.

I'm actually laughing through my tears writing that. Is that the greatest exit line or what? That is Hannah. Sweet. Nurturing. And with a streak of rebelliousness that can win wars. That streak makes me believe that she's going to survive this. Even better, she's going to thrive on her own. That gives me hope that I'm going to be okay too.

I have no idea what's going to happen next. Alanna says we can stay with her for as long as we need. But that can't last forever. We have to figure something out. We have to create a new life outside of our parents. What will that look like? It will be our brave new world. Emphasis on brave.

But first tomorrow. I have to get through tomorrow before I can think about what comes after.

Signed,
Mellie Rivers

March 25
Dusk
Dear Ms. Tilson,

In the end, it happened on Sunday morning, right around the time I would've been in church.

Daphne drove us. She picked us all up at Rosemary's house. I rode to the clinic sandwiched between Lise and Hannah, each of my hands twined in one of theirs. The storm was over—in more ways than one—and the sun had come out. I love sunlight after it snows. Everything sparkles.

I will always remember this day, I thought as we drove to the clinic.

Daphne made to turn into the alley that led to the underground garage, but I spoke up. "I want to go in through the front."

She slowed the car to a stop and turned to look at me. "Are you sure?"

Lise's brow furrowed. "It's not a good idea, Mellie. This is already hard enough."

"I know." I squeezed her fingers. "But I need to own this." I looked between her and Hannah. "I'm strong enough now."

"I'm going too," Alanna said. "About time I walked through the front doors of my own clinic."

I climbed out of the car after Lise, with Hannah behind me. There weren't that many protesters on a Sunday morning; probably because most of them were at church. Which is where I would be next Sunday. Maybe not at my family's church. Maybe a kinder, gentler church that welcomes everyone, and picks people up when they fall down.

The four protesters who were there saw us get out. They were mostly old ladies, their Bibles splayed out on their palms. A sign that read Every Life Is Precious leaned against their knees. One of them twisted a rosary in her fingers, rocking back and forth as she said the prayers.

"Your baby deserves a life," called out a gray-haired lady wearing a knitted hat with a gold angel pinned to it.

Lise must've felt me stiffen because she muttered "Don't engage," into my ear.

I couldn't help it.

I stopped and looked the woman in the eyes.

"So do I."

The women stared at me for a moment. The one saying the

rosary paused her praying. I pointed at myself, right at my heart. "My life is precious too. And I'm not going to sacrifice it for my rapist's baby."

It was as if I'd slapped them across the face. Some pro-lifers believe in exceptions in cases of rape, and I could see my words sinking in. Before any of them could speak, Lise led me away. I leaned into her and Hannah. I didn't need their strength—I had my own—but as long as they offered it, I was going to take it. I wasn't going to refuse anyone's help again.

The ironic thing is that it was over so fast. All these weeks of torture, and it turned out that making the decision was worse than the actual procedure.

Lise and Hannah waited in the lobby for me while Alanna took me back to the exam room. She'd given me something the night before to dilate my cervix, and when I got to the clinic, she gave me painkillers. I put on a soft cotton gown and climbed up onto the table, then fitted my feet in the stirrups. For a second, my chest tightened and I could feel the basement floor beneath me, hear his breathing above my ear…

Then the nurse, Maureen, offered her hand. "You squeeze as much as you need," she said. Alanna nodded, reassuring. There was nothing but kindness here. I was the most vulnerable I would ever be, and they would keep me safe.

"Cough," Alanna said. I did, feeling a little prick down there. "Just numbing your cervix," she said, and placed the syringe on the table next to her when she was finished. I squeezed Maureen's hand.

Alanna put a small tube with a suction device inside me and flipped the switch. A soft whirring noise filled the room. I squeezed Maureen's hand. It hurt the way bad cramps hurt during your period. I closed my eyes tight and waited for it to be over. I knew I had made the right choice, but that didn't make it easy.

I squeezed Maureen's hand tighter. With a steady and gentle touch, she wiped my tears.

After a few minutes, Alanna clicked off the machine. "It's done," she said.

A tremor went through me. Maybe it was the pain. Maybe it was relief. Maybe it was the angel wing brushing my cheek as the baby went up to heaven. Sobs racked my body. Alanna held me. I think she might have been crying too.

"It's over," she whispered, and I felt it, deep inside me. It really was over. My body belonged to me again.

Maureen and Alanna helped me into the recovery room, which felt more like a spa than a clinic. There were low lights, a Buddha's head waterfall in the corner, lots of pillows and blankets and magazines to read, juice and crackers on the tables next to the lounges. I was bleeding a lot, so I went to the bathroom to get a maxi pad, and then Alanna settled me in a lounge chair with a heating pad across my stomach. Lise and Hannah came in and sat with me. We didn't say anything. I wasn't sure there were words left to say, and I wanted quiet anyway, to listen to my own thoughts.

My own thoughts are this:

Having an abortion is an experience I would not wish on my worst enemy.

But if you have to go through one, it should be the way I did. Surrounded by love. Bolstered by support. Having your hand held and your tears wiped away by kind, gentle hands. Recovering in a room that is beautiful and comfortable, where your loved ones can be with you.

Those women protesting outside, they didn't know my story until I told them. All the other women who have abortions, we don't know their stories either. So we don't have the right to judge.

Now that you know my story, maybe you're judging me. Maybe you've got all sorts of ideas about what I should've done and what other choices I should've made.

You can think whatever you want.

I know I made the right choice.

Signed,

Mellie Rivers

March 29

Dear Ms. Tilson—

On Monday night there was one phone call. It was a hang-up, so I didn't think much of it. On Tuesday night there were three calls. Two were hang-ups. The third went like this:

Me: Hello?

Person on the other end: Is Alanna Grant there?

Me: Who's calling?

Asshole on the other end: Judgment Day. I'm coming for her.

Click.

On Wednesday night there were seven calls. A few were hang-ups, but most were like that last exchange. Last night there were fifteen calls. Today my mom disconnected the phone.

"Ignore it," my mom said. She looks freaked, Ms. Tilson. The owner of the clinic is stepping up security, for both the clinic and our house. The sheriff says he's going to send a patrol car by our house a few times a night. It doesn't make me feel that much better.

The thing is, we know who's behind the harassment, but we can't prove it.

It's Mayor Rivers or Pastor Talbot, or a collaborative effort between the two of them. Probably the latter. On Tuesday morning Delia Talbot hip-checked me on the way to homeroom, her long braid slapping me across the face. "What the hell?" I said. She ignored me and continued down the hall.

I followed her and cut her off before she could go into her classroom. I know I shouldn't have done it, I should have followed my escort training—*don't engage*—but anger was rising in me.

Delia stopped before she could run into me, but I was close enough to smell the shampoo she'd used on her hair that morning. "Do you have a problem with me, Delia?"

She blinked and looked around. Normally she has a couple of friends with her, but this morning she was alone. It was just her and me. "As a matter of fact, I do." Her eyes narrowed so that her whole face pinched into a mean expression. "I have a problem with the fact that your mother is a baby killer."

I've heard the protesters use that term all the time, but hearing it here, in school, in my face was different.

I leaned in close. Our noses were almost touching. "Well, I have a problem with the fact that your brother is a rapist."

Delia reared back, and for a second I really thought she was going to slap me. She must've thought better of it. Slapping me would result in her getting punished, and I was the guilty one in her mind.

We both stared at each other, breathing hard. I had no idea what was going on around us. There could've been a riot in that hallway and the two of us would still have been frozen, facing off across a gulf of pro-choice and anti-choice that I don't think will ever be bridged, at least not in my lifetime. I know with absolute certainty that I am on the right side, but so does she. I will never change my mind...and neither will she.

The whole week has been like this. People haven't said stuff to my face, but I've seen them stare, heard them whisper. Rowan and Cara have formed a shield around me—and so did Mellie when she came back to school on Wednesday. I can't hide behind them forever. I have to be my own shield.

I don't want to tell Mom about what's happening at school. She's already freaked out and I don't want to add to that.

But I have a feeling things are only going to get worse.

—Lise

April 27
Dear Ms. Tilson–

Here is a list of the reasons we are moving to New Mexico:

- After that first week, Mom disconnected our phone. Then calls started coming in on the cell phone—hers and mine.
- Every phone call is a variation on the same threat: that my mother will burn in Hell and they'll make sure she gets there soon. Tell me how someone who calls themselves pro-life thinks it's fine to threaten to kill someone?
- Almost daily we get a box on our doorstep. We don't open them. We call Sheriff Newman. One box had thirty-six severed dolls' heads in it. The last box we got had a bomb. Well, it looked like one and it was ticking. The Wolverton Police Department doesn't exactly have a bomb squad, but luckily there's an officer who used to defuse IEDs in Afghanistan and he came over. He took one look at the device and knew it was a fake. But still. SOMEONE PUT A FAKE BOMB ON OUR DOORSTEP.

- I opened my locker last week to find a baby doll hanging from a noose inside it. Besides being creepy, someone broke into my locker. Principal Conway acted concerned, but she said there was no way to find out who did it, and we should just let the matter drop. When Mom tried to call the superintendent about it, his assistant wouldn't even put her through. Conway and the superintendent, they both think I'm a troublemaker, a rabble-rouser, and now that they know about Mom, they don't even bother to hide their politics.
- Delia Talbot is waging a personal war against me. My clothes were stolen while I showered after gym class, I was followed around school by her horde of minions whispering "baby killer" behind my back, and Jason Bellows threw red paint at me. Again, Principal Conway has done exactly nothing about this.
- The underground garage at the clinic is no longer safe. Someone figured out how to hack into the control pad and decorated Mom's parking space with pictures of aborted fetuses (which were all photoshopped; aborted fetuses don't look like babies, which people should be smart enough to know). A security expert came out to reconfigure the system, but how long before the next hack?
- Sheriff Newman has had an officer stationed outside our house twenty-four-seven since the phone calls and boxes started arriving. But he can't keep someone there forever. He

can't spare the resources...and it's not like the mayor's office is going to increase his budget to protect my mom.

- Oh, yeah. And last week someone came into the clinic with a gun.

I'm sure you heard about that. It made the news.

The man didn't shoot anyone, which is what everyone has been fixating on. What they should focus on is how someone came into a medical office where women get health care and other hardworking people provide that care, and threatened to kill them all. It was over pretty quickly. Daphne and Jasmine are armed security, and they were able to defuse the situation.

That was the last straw.

Meanwhile, Brandon Talbot is walking around free. Well, not here in Wolverton. He left to do "missionary work" for the church in Africa the week after Mellie told her family what he did to her. I'm sure his dad sent him away, to protect the family from shame. It's not common knowledge about what happened to Mellie, but Hannah told enough people the truth of her broken engagement, so the story is out there. Still, he'll never serve time for what he did. I hope fate punishes him some other way.

I know I sound like I'm taking all of this in stride, but it's because all my anger has taken a new shape. I wear it as my armor. I have my own shield and sword, and I'm going to use it to fight these people, these laws, until things are better for women.

Because it feels as if the situation is getting worse. Mayor Rivers may not be elected yet, but he's already won. He's running Mom out of town, and the clinic is shutting down. The owners don't think it's safe here anymore. They're going to reopen it somewhere else, but that just means the women here have to travel farther to get their care.

So we're moving. This is my last entry on my last day of school. I'm going to turn in my journal to you this afternoon.

I don't want to leave Wolverton. I love it here. I love these mountains and the deep snow that comes in the winter, the flowers that grow on the mountainside in spring. I love Mellie, Cara, Rowan, and Rosemary. I love the red velvet cake at Marie's and the Christmas lights that are strung up across Main Street in December.

But more than all these things put together, I love my mom, and I need her to be safe.

Moving won't be all bad. Dad's girlfriend is going to have a baby. I'm going to have a half-sister. That's pretty cool. And we'll only be about an hour away from them, so maybe Dad and I can start to mend what was broken when he left. I think I understand him better now, because I've had the same fears as he must've had about Mom and her job.

Someday I'm going to come back to these mountains. I'm going to charge down into this valley with my sword and sweep away all the injustice that ever broke my heart. I'm going to leave shining cities on the horizon in my wake. Shining cities full of love and freedom.

Shining cities ruled by women.

—Lise

May 29

Dear Mellie—

It snowed last night and I thought of you. I didn't think it snowed this late in the year in Santa Fe, but Dad said it can, especially at night when it's cold and the wind blows down off the mountains. It's not like Colorado snow, though. Nothing is like Colorado snow.

I loved your last letter—and I love that we're writing letters to each other. Writing in those journals helped me too, and it's different to write a letter than an email. Emails are better for forwarding funny BuzzFeed lists or confirming dinner plans. Letters give deeper access to our hearts. I like to think we're bringing back the lost art of letter-writing, one heartfelt letter at a time.

I think I made a friend! She boards a horse at the stable where I've been riding a few times a week, and we've been going on rides together. She's showed me the trails with the best views. She goes to a different school than me, which kinda sucks. It's hard being "the new girl."

But I won't be the new girl forever, and it's so much better for Mom here. We still have to be cautious, but there are no underground garages, no fake names, no cars with tinted windows. There are still protesters, but the escorts usually outnumber them. I'm escorting here too, and I've rounded up some other girls from my high school to join me.

Dad's girlfriend, Amy, is getting big; the baby is due in September. Last weekend while I was visiting, I felt the baby kick. It was so cool! I could actually see her little foot through the skin of Amy's belly. She and I went to get mani-pedis together. I know I said she was annoying in my last letter, but I have to amend that. I think what I meant was overeager. She's definitely a little pushy when it comes to having a relationship with me, but that's because she wants to create a warm, loving home to bring her daughter into. And I admire that.

Over gelato after our mani-pedis, Amy told me she considered having an abortion when she found out she was pregnant. I couldn't believe it. Apparently she wasn't sure where she and Dad stood at the time, and she wasn't sure she was ready to be a single parent. I asked if Dad's opinion influenced her decision in any way. She said, "No, I didn't tell him about the baby until after I decided to keep it." Which is exactly what I would've done.

I'm so glad she made that decision, because

I'm so excited to have a sister, Mellie. I can't wait to rock the baby to sleep in the middle of the night like you did with Joanie. I'm going to be the best big sister there is. I'm going to be her Hannah.

How is Hannah, by the way? And how is the new apartment?! You barely mentioned it in your last letter, and hello, that's a big deal. I need details, girl! And how are Cara and Rowan? I hear from them all the time, but I want to know how they are from your perspective. I miss you guys so much that it's a physical ache, like something has been removed from my insides and I keep searching for it. Texting and FaceTiming every day doesn't cut it. Mom says I can come up to visit over the summer, so I hope there is a pullout couch for me to sleep on in that apartment.

Maybe someday you can come down here to

visit. I know money is tight for you and Hannah, but Mom's offer to pay for your ticket still stands. It would be so amazing. We could ride horses and roast marshmallows under the stars. You would not believe the night sky here. I've never seen so many stars, not even in Colorado where it feels as if you are so high up you can touch them. In New Mexico, it's like someone has pulled a magical cloak across the sky.

Sometimes when I lie on the back porch and look up at that sky, I think about you and me and how we were once two separate stars in the sky. Now we're part of the same constellation. Apart, we shine, but together, we're so much brighter.

Write back soon. And keep shining, my forever friend.

Love always,

—Lise

June 5

Dear Lise,

I almost wrote "Dear Ms. Tilson." Haha. I already turned that journal in because it was full. I've started another one. I think journal writing is second nature now. It's a product of that particular time in my life. There's my life BR (Before Rape) and my life AA (After Abortion). The time in between...I can't name it, but it is its own era, and I can count on two fingers the things that got me through that era: writing in that journal, and you.

I miss you too. SO MUCH. Every day I walk into school expecting to see you. Your locker hasn't been reassigned, and there's still a fragment of an old postcard stuck to the edge of the door. The postcard is bright blue with a speck of white, like a wide-open sky stretched over the tip of a snowy mountain. When I pass it, I feel hopeful. I know that sounds weird. But thinking about you always gives me hope. Hope that someday the world will be as you and I want it to be, not how it is.

Things at school have improved; people have moved on from the rumors that swirled around. And summer is almost here; people will forget about it come fall. I told Susanna the truth, because I wanted her to hear it from me instead of whatever lie she was going to hear from Delia. Although Delia has been conspicuously quiet. She leaves me alone and I leave her alone. Anyway, Susanna gave me a huge hug and told me she was sorry I had to go through all that I did. Then she said, "It's not the decision I would've made, but it's your choice." I just looked at her and said, "You can never know what decision you're going to make until you're in that situation." I'm glad she knows now...but I'm glad I didn't tell her before.

Cara, Rowan, and I eat lunch together every day. You wanted to know how they are... What can I say that they haven't already told you? They miss you like I miss you. I would definitely say Rowan is pining for you. I know you guys pseudo-broke up when you left, but trust me, that boy's heart is not ready to move on. Besides, what girl could live up to the impossible standard you have set? Cara has been teaching me to sew. We spent last Saturday at the fabric store, and then I made a skirt. The hem is a little uneven and the waist is lopsided, but still—I made it! Oh, and that hem was above my knee. I've been wearing a lot of skirts that end above my knees lately. Even Hannah wears shorter skirts now. On days when we both do, we look at each other and giggle like two little girls who've stolen the cookie jar and eaten all the cookies.

Hannah is now officially my guardian. Living with her is fun, though it has its ups and downs. We each keep to our own schedule, both of which are insanely busy. Hannah's gone back to school, and I'm working at the gallery most nights, plus taking private drawing lessons with Rosemary. We have our own rooms at the new apartment (yes, there is a pullout couch), so we can retreat to our separate sanctuaries. It is so different than life at home (our old home), so it's an adjustment to live in the quiet with one's own thoughts.

But every couple of days we'll come together, like we're starved for each other's company, and we'll talk. About everything, about life, about the most mundane things that we now have to think about since we moved out, like who is picking up more toilet paper. Sometimes, rarely, we talk about HIM. He's a shared pain. What she feels, I feel. Even though he didn't rape her too, what he did to me he did to her.

I'm still going to the rape survivor group at the community center every week. Even on the nights when I don't speak, it's good to sit and listen. To know that someone else went through what I did. To know I'm not alone. It's funny, I thought after I had the abortion and my family deserted me, I would feel so alone. I think that was part of what I was really afraid of. But the last couple months I've felt less alone than I did in my parents' house. Being surrounded by all those people and unable to be my true self...that was far lonelier.

Speaking of my parents, I haven't talked to them. Bethany manages to sneak over a couple of times a week. Dad doesn't know. I think Mom might. I think Mom misses us, or maybe even regrets what happened, but she's never going to go against Dad. Bethany says that Ruth and Joanie ask about us all the time, and one time Dad yelled, "They're dead to us!" which made the girls cry.

I cried a little myself when she told me that. Maybe someday I can forgive Mom, but I can never forgive Dad. Not because of what he did to me, but for what he did to your mom. For exposing her. For effectively driving you out of town. For not including her life in the "life" that the "pro-life" movement so zealously believes in.

I miss Ruth and Joanie. The ache for them in my chest comes and goes. Bethany says she's going to try to bring them to visit sometime. I hope when they're older, I can tell them my side of the story, and they can decide how they feel for themselves.

I'm still figuring out what comes next in my story, and I've realized that's okay. I don't need to have the whole story all figured out now, or in the next year or five years or ten years. I'll probably be figuring it out for as long as I live. I've realized that people can change throughout their life—and should change. People can think they're pro-life and then something happens to them, or to someone they love, and they discover they were pro-choice all along. People can believe they will get married at twenty-two and have babies only to decide that's not what they want out of life after all. People can start down one path and then go off it, forging a new path no one has ever been down.

What I discovered writing in that journal are my innermost thoughts. I never knew them before. But putting them on paper helped me uncover them. It helped me see <u>me</u> for who I really am, at this moment in time, at this part of my life.

So this is who I am: the Mellie you helped. I am full of flaws that I'm not afraid for the world to see. I'm Mayor Rivers's daughter, who no longer stands behind him. I still get straight As, but my hemlines have been raised and my hair has been cut above my shoulders and dyed pink. I still go to church on Sunday, but I've started attending the Unitarian Universalist church, which has a rainbow flag hanging outside. I don't do everything right, but I no longer feel like I <u>have</u> to. I've been through some version of Hell, but I've come out the other side.

I'm a survivor.

I'm sixteen, and I've had an abortion. There are a whole lot of people in this world who love me, and someday I'll find someone to love me the same way that Rowan loves you. I can't change what happened to me, but it's like everything had to get stripped away so the real me could be revealed, and who I am now is so much more than who I was.

I'll come to New Mexico this summer. I'm not too proud to let your mom pay for my ticket. We can lie under that big, wide sky. We'll reach our hands up to the stars and maybe, just maybe, we'll touch them.

Love,
Mellie

AUTHOR'S NOTE

From every corner of my life, they came to me. They told me their stories in hushed or matter-of-fact tones, over coffee, over drinks, in the beauty salon, through Facebook messages, standing on a lawn watching our children play, in office break rooms.

Women I knew, women I loved and cared for deeply, women who'd had abortions.

People would ask me all the time, "What are you writing now?" I'd be honest and say, "I'm writing a book about abortion." And inevitably there would be the confession: "I had one."

So many of these women I knew for a long time, yet I never knew this about them.

And the truth is, someone you know, someone you love, has had an abortion.

Abortion is not, should not be, a political issue. This is an emotional health decision that so many women have to make—and they shouldn't have to make it in secret or in shame. One woman I spoke with told me I was only the third person—including the father—she'd told about her abortion. Not even her family knew. Imagine not being able to tell your family about the hardest decision you've ever made.

I've tried to capture that aspect of abortion in this book. The deep, gut-wrenching emotion of the decision-making process. I hope I've succeeded.

I have always been pro-choice, but before I started working on this novel, I think I would've judged these women without even realizing I was doing it. I would've thought something like, *I would never get myself into that situation* or *I would make a different choice.* But writing this novel taught me you can never truly know what you would do in a certain situation until you are in it, and we can't judge anyone for making a choice under circumstances that we haven't experienced.

No one wants to have an abortion. No one waltzes into a clinic whistling a happy tune. It is the most agonizing decision a woman may ever have to make. And anyone who accuses women of using abortion as birth control needs to look at the underlying issues. Can she afford birth control? Does she live three hundred miles from the closest clinic and work two jobs and can't drive that far for the appointment to get a prescription for birth control? Does her abusive boyfriend refuse to wear a condom?

Until we walk in someone else's shoes, we cannot know. We cannot judge.

But what we can do is examine the fact that the maternal

mortality rate has skyrocketed in the United States, so much so that we have the most pregnancy-related deaths in any developed nation. We are the only country in the developed world where the number of women who die in childbirth has actually risen in the last twenty-five years. That is a direct result of a lack of access to reproductive health care, to birth control, and to abortions. It is also a symptom of a culture that places more value on the life of a fetus than the life of its mother.

Let us all be pro-life—the *real* meaning of pro-life. Let us be in favor of the whole life of a woman, not just her role as a mother, but everything else she might accomplish. Let us be for life coming into the world when it is wanted, and cared for emotionally and financially. Let us support the entire life of that child from birth to death.

Let us encourage women to make the decision that is best for them, instead of shaming them. Let our bodies be our own, not a political battleground. Let us have the same autonomy over our bodies that men have. Let us be free—to choose, to share our stories, and to live.

RESOURCES

If you have been abused or sexually assaulted, RAINN can help. Contact the National Sexual Assault Hotline at (800) 656-HOPE or visit their website at rainn.org.

For comprehensive reproductive health care, including Pap smears, annual check-ups, birth control, breast cancer screenings, prenatal care, and abortion services, visit your local Planned Parenthood. Find a health center online at plannedparenthood.org or call (800) 230-PLAN.

To find out about abortion restrictions in your state, visit guttmacher.org or plannedparenthood.org.

READING GROUP GUIDE

1. At the beginning of the story, Lise picks up on clues in Mellie's behavior that lead her to believe something is wrong. Even though Mellie tells her to leave her alone, Lise persists. At what point would you have given up on getting someone to open up to you? Do you think Lise pushed too hard?

2. When Mellie finally opens up to Lise, she's relieved and also surprised that she feels comfortable confiding in Lise. Is there a person in your life who you turn to? Are there people in your life who you care about, but whom you wouldn't be willing to trust with your confidence?

3. One of the main themes of the book is choice. We all have the right to make our own choices for ourselves. Do you agree with Mellie's choice? Do you agree with Lise's choice to help Mellie no matter what?

4. Alanna's safety is one of Lise's top priorities, but in the end, she and Alanna sacrifice their safety to help Mellie. Would you have done the same? What lengths would you go to in order to protect the people you love?

5. If one of your teachers gave you a journal to write in, would you do it? How much of your innermost self would you expose on the page, knowing that someone else is going to read it?

6. Throughout the book, Mellie is determined not to tell her parents the truth about what happened to her, supposedly to protect her sister. Do you think she should have told them right away? How do you think the story would have changed if she'd opened up to them—or a teacher or another responsible adult—in the first place?

7. Do you agree with how Mellie's parents handled her situation? If you were a parent, how do you think you would handle it?

8. Thirty-nine out of the fifty United States have some kind of parental consent or notification law if an underage girl wants to have an abortion. Do you agree that states should have parental permission and/or notification laws? What are the advantages and disadvantages of such a law?

9. The goal of the anti-choice movement is to reduce abortions by limiting access. The goal of the pro-choice movement is to reduce abortions by expanding access to birth control and reproductive health care. Which approach do you think is more effective? Is there another option to consider? If so, what?

10. Mellie begins the book sharing the beliefs her parents taught her, but by the end of the book, she has a different perspective. What do you think changed her beliefs? Do you think she was influenced by Lise's beliefs or her own experience?

11. At the end of the book, Lise decides she wants to pursue a career in politics. Do you think that is a good way to effect change? Is there an issue you would like to see changed in your community, and how would you effect that change?

12. Toward the beginning of the book, Lise thinks she is ready to have sex with Rowan, but her experience with Mellie makes her rethink her decision. If you were Lise's friend and she wanted to talk through this decision, how would you advise her?

13. What do you think Mellie and Lise do with their lives after the book ends? How do you think this experience changed them?

14. Is there a villain in this book? Who do you think it is? Why?

15. Do you think it is possible to be friends with someone who has completely different beliefs than you? How can those differences strengthen or weaken a friendship?

ACKNOWLEDGMENTS

There are a lot of people without whom my books and my writing would not happen, and to them I am forever grateful.

To my agent, my tireless champion, Irene Goodman, I owe so much gratitude that there is not enough gratitude in the world to cover my debt. Thank you for giving me the kernel of the idea for this story, and then encouraging me all along the way. Thank you for fighting for it with as much passion as I had. Thank you for being my anchor for the last thirteen years, and please don't ever retire because I will be lost without you.

To my editor, Annette Pollert-Morgan, for seemingly reading my mind and being on the same page (pun intended!) with me about what this book needed to be. Thank you for your guidance in making this book the strongest possible version of itself. Most of all, thank you for allowing me to say what I wanted to say, and pushing me to make my voice stronger.

To Cassie Gutman, my production editor, and Christa Desir, my copyeditor, for your incredibly astute notes, for making every word of this book matter, and for hearting my *Parks and Rec* and *Game of Thrones* references. To the entire Sourcebooks team, especially Sarah Kasman, Steve Geck, and Todd Stocke, for supporting this book and for giving me the space and breadth I needed to write it.

Thank you so much to my early readers Michelle Levy and Lizzie Andrews for your notes, advice, and encouragement. A very special thank-you to my sensitivity reader and friend Michelle Grondine for your very loving notes and for being such a strong, outspoken advocate for sexual assault survivors.

A huge bourbon barrel of thanks to the Los Angeles writing community, whose enduring support and love is a source of strength and much-needed levity. Nobody has more fun than a bunch of writers when they get together. Special thanks to Robin Reul, Gretchen McNeil, Jen Klein, Kathy Kottaras, Amy Spalding, Tracy Holczer, Catherine Linka, Charlotte Huang, Elana K. Arnold, Mary McCoy, and Jen Brody for being some of the best pals a girl could ever ask for.

To my twin brain, my soul sister, Romina (Russell) Garber—where would I be without you? One sad sack drinking coffee at Le Pain Quotidien all alone. Your friendship means the world to me, and your support throughout the writing of this book kept me sane.

To my best big sister, Tanya, for always, always being on my side.

To Chris and Emilia, who sustain me. I can do anything because I have you.

To all the women who spoke to me about their abortion experiences: Danielle, Gina, Connie, Heather, Jen, and other friends: I hope you know what a gift you gave me by sharing your stories. This book is for you.

And lastly, to all the women and girls out there who are making this decision right now: I see you. I support you. And you are not alone.

ABOUT THE AUTHOR

Nicole Maggi wrote her first story in third grade about a rainbow and a unicorn. She is the author of *The Forgetting*, a 2016 International Thriller Writers Thriller Award finalist, and the Twin Willows Trilogy, which *VOYA* called "reminiscent of *Twilight* and Harry Potter." Visit her at nicolemaggi.com.